THE SURVIVALIST SAGA CONTINUES by Sharon Ahern

Once again the Rourkes must face the trials and tribulations associated with being the First Family of the Entire World. Imagine the scrutiny today's press puts on one of our music or media icons and then multiply that intense examination extended to the entire Rourke clan. Sarah is married to Wolfgang Mann, who is none other than the President of New Germany. She shares the limelight with her husband and the danger associated with the office such as disapproving factions and terrorists. Remember the old days, around six hundred and fifty years ago, when all Sarah wanted was a peaceful existence with her family and the time to write and illustrate children's books?

Michael Rourke, so much like his father, wants to lead his fellow Americans away from the current liberal agenda prevalent in the United States and restore a more responsible government that is accountable to its people. After an ugly political campaign, he rises up out of the muck as the new President. Michael will be dealing with the usual pressures of the office; people who think he is a psychological killer maniac, those who think his former Russian KGB agent wife is an unsuitable First Lady and, illegal aliens from outer space who want to take over the planet.

No matter how far into the future you travel, some things never change; there will always be just some news twists to age old situations, but, as John Thomas Rourke is wont to say, "It always pays to plan ahead."

Sharon

Books in The Survivalist Series by Jerry Ahern

#1: Total War
#2: The Nightmare Begins
#3: The Quest
#4: The Doomsayer
#5: The Web
#6: The Savage Horde
#7: The Prophet
#8: The End is Coming
#9: Earth Fire
#10: The Awakening
#11: The Reprisal
#12: The Rebellion
#13: Pursuit
#14: The Terror
#15: Overlord

Mid-Wake
#16: The Arsenal
#17: The Ordeal
#18: The Struggle
#19: Final Rain
#20: Firestorm
#21: To End All War
The Legend
#22: Brutal Conquest
#23: Call To Battle
#24: Blood Assassins
#25: War Mountain
#26: Countdown
#27: Death Watch

Books in The Survivalist Series by
Jerry Ahern, Sharon Ahern and Bob Anderson
#30: The Inheritors of the Earth
#31: Earth Shine
The Shades of Love (Short Story)

Books by Bob Anderson
Sarge, What Now?
Anderson's Rules
Grandfather Speaks

TAC Leader Series
#1 What Honor Requires
#2 Night Hawks
#3 Retribution

THE SURVIVALIST

#31

EARTH SHINE

SPEAKING VOLUMES, LLC
NAPLES, FLORIDA
2013

THE SURVIVALIST
#31 EARTH SHINE

ISBN 978-1-62815-085-8

Editorial contributions and editorial assistance by Pamela Anderson, Allan Cole.

THE SURVIVALIST

#31

Earth Shine

Jerry Ahern
Sharon Ahern
Bob Anderson

Prologue

The three heavy armored black SUVs negotiated Honolulu noontime traffic before heading east out of town. President of the United States (POTUS), Michael Rourke, was in the second vehicle receiving a briefing from the head of his security detail. The energy blast vaporized the right front quarter panel of the lead vehicle, and it slammed the vehicle a dozen feet to the left causing it to careen through the guard rail and down the steep incline. More through luck than any actual skill, it did not roll over.

The passenger in the right front passenger seat had died as a result of the greenish energy bolt's impact. The driver and the folks in the back seat were slammed violently to the left with the air bags deploying. Those in the back seat were knocked unconscious.

The driver was stunned and operating more on reflexes as he tried to keep the vehicle upright when a tree suddenly appeared in the driver's vision; the vehicle's front end caught it dead center, crumpling the remainder of the front end beyond recognition. While the puncture proof gas tanks held, gas line connections to the vehicle's motor were ripped lose, and the smell of gasoline permeated the vehicle. Smoke and flames began to creep visibly from under the crumpled hood.

Chapter One

John Thomas Rourke was both angry and bothered. A coordinated attack by ground and air forces had hit the Capital Building in Honolulu during his son Michael's inauguration as President. Yet, as bad as that attack had been, and it had been bad, it could have been far worse. Even with the horrendous death on the ground, the fact several entire sections of Honolulu had been destroyed, it could and should have been far worse; that was the part that bothered Rourke most. Why wasn't it?

Emma had stabilized after almost going into labor; their unborn child was safe and expected to be able to be carried to full term. Michael and Natalia had survived. Rourke's own injuries were comparatively minor. The burns on his left hand and arm were healing; nerve damage to that limb was not a threat. Luckily, the energy blast had not affected his right hand, and he had been able to neutralize the enemy sniper with three shots from his Detonics .45.

Smoke rose over the city from the crashes of four American fighters, an airliner, two American news choppers, and three of the enemy aircraft. The initial reports of enemy ground forces were later determined to be false and the result of "friendly fire" incidents between military and police units mistaking each other for the enemy; there were several casualties on both sides.

The resulting crashes were responsible for over 1,200 deaths on the ground, either from falling debris, shrapnel from explosions, or fire. The fires devastated a large section of the downtown area and a suburban neighborhood on the outskirts of town. The major fires had burned longer than originally expected. It took three days for them to be extinguished rather than the anticipated couple of hours. Flaming debris had been scattered from one end of the Capital to the other.

The airliner crash killed all 228 onboard and sprayed hundreds of gallons of flaming jet fuel across one subdivision. Twenty-seven homes and one school had been incinerated. Within the homes, 17 parents and 21 children below school age perished.

In the school, 1,018 students and teachers suffocated when the fire sucked the oxygen out of the school. The only survivors were the football team, their coaches, band members, and sponsors who were at a neighboring school preparing for a championship game.

Of the four attacking enemy aircraft, which at this stage remained identified as unidentified flying objects, three had been shot down and one was missing. Those crash sites were declared National Security Areas, and investigators were still pouring over them. Strangely, it had been determined the pilots for those crafts appeared to be human.

Stranger still was the fact that all three possessed the same face, that of Captain Dodd, one of the original Eden Project astronauts. This was the second time in just a few months one of Dodd's reincarnations had been encountered.

Following his inauguration, Michael's first act as the new American President had been to break the jaw of his former opponent Phillip Greene on national TV. President Rourke had then declared the state of Hawaii a National Disaster. In the affected areas, teams had evacuated building occupants along evacuation routes to primary assembly points and redirected building occupants to stairs and exits away from the fire. Contingency plans for hazardous material spills or releases, nuclear power plant incidents, transportation accidents, and everything else one could imagine had been activated.

One of his next acts was to change a policy for the presidential security detail. Before his election, Michael and Natalia had been summoned for a meeting with President Arthur Hooks and Vice-President Benjamin Richardson. The presidential security detail apologized, but their personal weapons had to be temporarily surrendered. Natalia had asked him, "If you win the Presidency, will you change that policy?" He had just made that change; it would be one of many to come.

The first 48 hours were the worst. Reports had been spotty and inaccurate. Initial responders were met with devastation and death. Those who had died quickly from the flames of incineration and suffocation resulting from the fire storms had been lucky. Those trapped under tons of collapsed buildings had taken days to die in slow agony without water, without food and totally alone.

Even before the Night of the War, Honolulu, located on the southeastern shore of the island of O'ahu, was the southernmost major U.S. city. King Kamehameha the First conquered his enemies and moved his court in 1809 to what is now downtown Honolulu. In the old Hawaiian language, Honolulu meant "sheltered bay" or "place of shelter." Three weeks ago, on the day of Michael's inauguration and as on December 7, 1941, Honolulu had proved to be neither.

Chapter Two

Captain Dodd's clone had escaped the aerial dog fight undetected, all according to plan. In the midst of the "fog of war," he had dropped to tree level after zipping through a cover of heavy smoke, thus escaping the radar tracking of the American forces. His Creator, commonly referred to as a member of an alien race or more accurately an Extraterrestrial Biological Entity or EBE, had monitored the battle and the loss of the other three UFO crafts. The attack had never been planned to be a successful kill shot against the government; it had simply been a distraction—a very successful distraction.

Dodd had landed in part of what remained of the Waiāhole Forest Reserve area, north of the capital city of Honolulu. Dodd's landing site had been prepared ahead of time. His egg-shaped craft was now housed in a tunnel complex that had formed the abandoned Waiāhole Ditch and Tunnel System. The craft was about 15 feet long, not quite as wide, and about 6 feet high. It had no windows, portholes, or wings.

This tunnel system was also the location of Dodd's forces, 100 of his companion cloned members of the original Eden Project's Shuttle Mission. The northern leg of the complex, slightly over two miles long, connects with side tunnels that come in from different directions and specifically the Kahana, Waikane, Waianu, and Waiāhole valleys.

Several historical and newspaper reports that survived the Night of the War identified that "within this system, the original railroad track remained and was used to facilitate movement of personnel and equipment. During construction, a steam engine used the track to haul debris from the main tunnel area down to the bay, a distance of 10 miles, where an ocean pier was constructed." The opening to each tunnel was now hidden by something called counter-illuminated camouflage that created an invisibility cloak or a force field, assuming the colors and textures of its surroundings.

In early twentieth century, over 6,004 exotic trees of molave, mahogany, and tulipwood had been planted. Only the mahogany and tulipwood had survived the Night of the War; they now proliferated in the area. It was no longer a commonly visited area; this meant no one else was aware that Dodd's encampment existed in the Waiāhole.

This version of Captain Dodd had been given the designation of Alpha-5 by his Coalition Creator, the same that had created the last Captain Dodd. The Creator had determined some degree of "military" organization was necessary for this operation to function properly. Alpha-5 and the rest of the clones had the original DNA of their original counterparts, but at the same time, there had been "modifications." The Creator had determined the failures of the other Dodd's had been primarily due to the suppression of their individual psyches.

Those experimentations had proven that, by sublimating areas of their human brains, it had limited their abilities to function. The Creator determined the mental functions of this species were intertwined with its senses and physicality. The suppression of those elements had greatly reduced the efficiency of each of the clones.

*****

Paul Rubenstein and Annie had been tangled up outside of the capital building parameter having arrived late for the ceremonies due to a flat tire Paul had been forced to change. Had that flat not occurred, they would have been at ground zero of the attack; he still didn't know whether to curse the flat or offer thanks that it had occurred.

Throughout his early exploits with John Thomas Rourke, Paul had endeavored to maintain a written history of their adventures. However, by the very nature of those battles, he kept losing his notebooks. Long after the Night of the War, he thought about trying to record the adventures on audio tape; it had been a start but not a great one. He tried to maintain that practice following the first cryogenic sleep. After John and Sarah were nearly killed by Dietrich Zimmer and before the entire Rourke family had entered the second sleep, he had again begun to chronicle those exploits but had never compiled everything together.

These days, Paul Rubenstein, the former junior editor for a trade magazine publisher, was accepted as a serious writer. He had been 28 years old and dying of boredom when Rourke had accepted him as a friend and partner. On their second day together so long ago, he had told John, "Two days ago, I needed help. Today—now I'm helping."

It was John Michael's idea, Paul and Annie's 14-year-old son, to finish the diary project. One report had falsely claimed that Col Karamatsov had been killed by John Rourke as the conflagration of the atmosphere approached the Retreat. The individual killed had in fact been a Colonel Rozhdestvenskiy; over the years, a lot of the "facts" had been changed or forgotten and some of the real stories simply lost. By the time Rourke and the "family" had awakened, their history had been effectively supplemented and occasionally even reinvented.

John Michael had realized the "history of the Rourke family" he was learning in school was very different from the history he was learning at home. During the second sleep, the world had thought the Rourke family, including Paul and Annie, had died. Their story remained fresh in the minds of those who had known them prior to the attack in Eden City, and many unintentional liberties were taken by well-meaning "historians." They had been romanticized to the roles of near gods, which they weren't. Awakening from the second sleep, they found themselves lauded as heroes and "national treasures" thought lost to history.

After the second awakening, there were countless battles and intrigues, not to mention family drama. When things had finally settled, the family structure had changed even more, but over the next nearly two decades, the "reality" of stories of John Thomas, Emma, Sarah, Wolfgang Mann, Michael, Natalia, Paul, and Annie continued to miss the mark. After one high school history lesson, John Michael had talked to his dad about the inaccuracies.

"Dad, no one knows the truth about the Rourkes. The teachers, and even the kids, think of us as 'special,' and it bugs me. I'm just a kid like my classmates, but our history books make the whole family into people we're not. Tell me the truth about what you, Mom, my grandparents, Uncle Michael, and Natalia really did."

That was the moment Paul Rubenstein knew the diary project was back on the front burner. He located his old tape recordings and had them transferred to a computer disc, beginning the process of cleaning up and catching up the story of the Rourke family. In recent days, Paul had come to think it would always be a "work in progress;" the story of the Rourke's was changing, yet again.

Part of that process was to obtain pictures and biographies on some of the key characters in that story, including the 115 members of the Eden Project. He now realized the story he and his family and friends had lived would take several volumes to make it complete. To adequately focus his activities on his "diary," he had a "secret weapon"—Amanda Welch, PhD candidate at the University of Mid-Wake, the oldest surviving academic institution on Earth located at Mid-Wake beneath the Pacific Ocean.

Amanda's lifelong passion—genealogy—coupled with the fact she was descended from one of the original Eden Project cadre and that her thesis was on theoretical astrophysics, had driven the research on her dissertation.

As part of the work, she had been examining the electronic logs of the original Eden Project 500-year voyage when she had discovered the "anomaly." As impossible as it had seemed, the Project had remained in a geosynchronous orbit around something—she had no idea what—for nearly three terrestrial years; then, it resumed its journey as if nothing had happened. Her professor, Doctor Emil Culbertson, had cautioned her against going public with such a report; "You'll end a promising career before it even gets started."

However, after the attack on John and Emma Rourke and the capture—however short lived—of one of Captain Timothy Dodd's clones during the "Fight in the Forest," there was now incontrovertible proof the Eden Project personnel, while traveling in cryogenic sleep through the void of space, had not only been observed, but their ships had been waylaid and visited by intelligent beings from another solar system, creatures far in advance of humankind. After being studied, examined, and experimented on for three years, the Eden Project had been sent along on its way. Amanda had the only complete set of dossiers and original photos for each of the original Eden Project crew members.

Chapter Three

Tim Shaw, John Rourke's father-in-law, was tired. Barefoot with a dirty t-shirt and old running shorts, he sat at the kitchen table looking more like a bum than a professional police detective; he didn't smell very good either. He was in the last weeks of his career as a cop, and it was telling on him. He and his son Eddie were killing a bottle of Single Malt Scotch. "Won't be long now, Son," the elder Shaw said for about the fifteenth time in the last two hours.

"Dad," Eddie reiterated for about the fifteenth time in the same hours, "you've got to snap outta this. You ought to be celebrating. You've made it almost all the way. You've had a great career, and you should be planning for retirement, not dreading it."

"So you've said," Tim came back. "But, here's my problem; so much of who I am has been tied to what I do. I've been a cop most of my adult life. You and Emma are grown with your own families; your Mom has been dead for years. Hell, I have grandkids about ready to graduate. What have I got to show for it all, a bunch of citations and these two pistols?" He slid the stainless slab-sided Lancer reproduction of a Colt Model 1911 .45 on the coffee table, but his version held 13 rounds in a double stack magazine instead of 7 or 8.

Next to it, he laid Lancer's version of a Smith and Wesson .38 Centennial snub nose revolver on the table between them. The five-shot revolver had been made by Smith & Wesson on the "J-Frame" but had a fully enclosed hammer that made it a double action only. Its swing-out cylinder was rated for .38 Special +P ammo. While mechanically perfect, years of use had imprinted both with character, battle scars, and holster wear.

This conversation had been going on, back and forth between them for the last six weeks. Each time it came up, Eddie saw the tension and anxiety from his father had moved to a new and higher level. He knew once a cop retired, if he didn't have something to grasp on to, that cop would become more and more withdrawn and deeper and deeper into a bottle. Suicide after retirement often seemed like the only way to reestablish control, and too many times, far too many times, the retired cop would simply "eat his gun."

An hour later, the Scotch was gone, and he threw a blanket over his dad who had passed out on the couch. When he climbed into his electric powered car, he called his sister Emma. "Sis, we need to talk; this thing with Dad is getting more serious. Can I swing over and talk to you and John for a few minutes?" Twenty minutes later, he pulled up at Rourke's beachfront house.

Rourke opened the door and asked, "Ed, what's going on?" He ushered his brother-in-law out on the patio.

"John, I'm really starting to get concerned about Dad," Eddie said rubbing his face so Rourke wouldn't notice the fact that tears had welled up in his eyes. "This retirement thing is really starting to settle on him. He's depressed; he feels used up and that he has nothing to contribute any longer. Once he loses his badge, he feels he will lose his identity."

Emma brought coffee out for them, and the three contemplated what might be done to avoid a tragedy, if anything. After an hour of discussion, Rourke excused himself and went inside to make a phone call. "I wished his relationship with Linda had panned out," Emma said. "He was happy for those few months; when she was killed, it was like the bottom fell out of him."

"I know," Eddie said. "The bottom is out of him, and the walls are falling in on him. He has got to find something to commit to Sis, or he's not going to come out of this." Having said that, the conversation just died, and the two simply sipped at their coffee. Neither had an answer; they didn't even have questions.

Rourke came back out, "Okay, try this on for size. I just spoke with Michael and told him our fears. He told me he was in the process of reworking the Secret Service protection coverage and duties. He asked if I thought your dad would be interested in that."

"John, if Dad thinks this is a handout... If he thinks this is just a gesture from the family, he'll turn it down. However," Emma said, "if he sees this as an opportunity, a real opportunity and a challenge, I think he'll jump on it. It will all be in the presentation."

Eddie nodded, "We'll have to carefully 'arrange' this, and he can't know we were directly involved."

"Let me and Michael handle that," Rourke said. "I have a couple of ideas."

*****

Dr. Fred Williams, head of the Mid-Wake Research Institute, had agreed to meet with John Rourke and The Keeper in his office. Rourke had requested the meeting; he had an idea he wanted to get clarification on. "So Dr. Williams, The Keeper has said the war with the alien EBEs was over chlorophyll," Rourke began. "Is my idea feasible?"

Williams shucked his suit coat and loosened his tie, pondering for a moment. "Theoretically, yes. It is possible to synthesize chlorophyll. The question becomes, is it possible to synthesize the amounts you're talking about? I believe it was in 1967 that the last remaining stereo chemical elucidation was completed by Ian Fleming."

"Ian Fleming," Rourke said. "I only know of one Ian Fleming; I know he was a very accomplished guy, but I had no idea he was into chemistry also."

Williams chuckled and turned to his bookshelf, scanned the collection before selecting one particular dusty and worn volume entitled *Pericyclic Reactions* part of the Oxford Chemistry Primers, and referred to it. "Wrong Ian Fleming, I suspect you're thinking of the writer who created James Bond. That was Ian Lancaster Fleming. The chemist, Ian Fleming, was a twentieth century organic chemist. Both were English, but my Fleming was a professor emeritus of the University of Cambridge and an emeritus fellow of Pembroke College, Cambridge."

"Fleming, my Fleming, was the first to determine the full structure of chlorophyll. He made major contributions to the use of organosilicon compounds for stereospecific syntheses, reactions, which have found application in the synthesis of natural compounds. He also was a prolific author, writing a number of textbooks and influential review articles."

"Your Fleming worked in British Naval Intelligence during World War II. He was involved in the planning stages of Operation Mincemeat and Operation Golden Eye. His wartime service and his career as a journalist provided much of the background, detail, and depth of the James Bond novels."

"Dr. Williams," The Keeper began with a smile. "Now that we have the Flemings sorted out, will Dr. Rourke's plan work?"

Williams nodded, "Sir, I think it will." Williams turned and pulled a book off the shelf; he flipped pages until he discovered what he was looking for, then he quoted, "The first step is the creation of porphyrins. These are a group of organic compounds, many naturally occurring. The porphyrins are heterocyclic ring structures that include four pyrrole rings joined together through methylene bridges."

"The most abundant porphyrins in nature are found in hemoglobin and the chlorophylls. In the center of porphyrins, a metal atom binds to the nitrogen atoms of the pyrrole units. In heme, this atom is iron; in chlorophyll, the metal atom is magnesium. The main 'application' of porphyrins is their role in supporting aerobic life. Porphyrins have been evaluated in the context of photodynamic therapy since they strongly absorb light, which is then converted to energy and heat in the illuminated areas."

He closed the book, flipped it on the desk, and continued, "It is more of an industrial concern at the level of produced material you want; the chemistry aspect is actually fairly simple and straightforward. However, to my knowledge, there is not a facility in the world capable of doing it at present."

"Could one be built?" The Keeper asked. "You must understand it is our opinion the immediate goal of the aliens is to alter the Earth's atmosphere, possibly radically increasing methane and thus depleting oxygen to the point where irreparable brain damage is incurred. Thus, they would have control of all but mindless slaves to mine and otherwise rape the planet, leaving the new base the aliens will establish secure against rebellion."

"They would do this by displacing oxygen and lowering levels below 18%, getting close to 6%, below which would result in death. This could be accomplished by increasing microbial populations and releasing already existing methane into the atmosphere through global wildfires. Before, when the aliens all but wiped out the protohumans, they didn't care about what they could take from the planet; they merely wanted to destroy a potential rival."

"I think one of the reasons is also that the aliens cannot last for long periods in our atmosphere; that's one of the reasons they need the clones. In the intervening millennia, the aliens have come to realize they need what can be plundered from Earth and all but mindless humans to provide it. We have to alter the equation in our favor, so, I ask you again. Can what John Rourke's hypothesis describes be built?"

"Sir, with sufficient financial resources, manpower, and time, almost anything can be," Dr. Williams said.

"That, sir, is the problem," Rourke said. "I don't know how much time we have."

Chapter Four

"It is difficult for people to imagine geological time; people live on another scale of time entirely," The Keeper said. "We cannot comprehend 'infinity' because we live in a 'finite' world, and within 'finite' time, people are unable to imagine the meaning of 80 million years. We knew that, geologically, Earth was locked in an inescapable series of events that were going to result in a shift of the magnetic poles, geological upheavals, and climatic changes that would last for eons. We had come to realize we had neither the power to destroy the planet nor to save it, but we reasoned we did have the power to save ourselves."

Dr. Williams nodded gravely, "That had to be a sobering decision."

The Keeper responded, "It was. We realized we could not evacuate the entire planet with its myriad of life forms. It may seem rather calculating, but my people understand evolution is simply the result of life escaping all barriers. Life breaks free. Life expands into new directions, painfully, tragically, and perhaps even dangerously, but life finds a way. Biological creatures are fluid; they only seem stable. They're not based on the time frame they are being observed in. For those short segments of reality, change is not observable. Increase the time frames, and it becomes observable. The reality is that everything is in constant movement, constantly changing."

"A biological generation is defined as 'The linear transition from one parent to one offspring.' In humans, the biological generation does not have a standard length of time, but there are limits. A dynamic generation is a concept used by anthropologists; it is similar to the biological generation but applied more broadly across a group of people. These methods of reckoning generations have to do more with the relationships between people than actual passage of time."

"Since our departure, earth has seen between 1,600 and 2,000 generations of humans; we are only in our second. How long is a generation, you ask? This short answer is 25 years, but a generation ago it was 20 years. The long answer is that it depends on what you mean by generation. More broadly speaking, humans have identifiable, meaningful, generation-related terminology and cultural concepts in many but not all societies, and when it does occur, it is more common to find the concept in age-graded societies or societies in which marriage arrangements are fairly strictly enforced, or at least strongly hoped for by the ascending generation."

"The way your society is structured, what you call science, developed very differently than ours. Science cannot help us decide what to do with this world or how to live in it. Your science made your 'nuclear reactor,' but it could not tell you not to build it. Your science could make pesticide but could not tell you not to use it; as a result, your world was polluted in fundamental ways—air, water, and land—because of ungovernable science. The ability to predict unfortunate outcomes is based on the ability to keep track of things. Observation and discovery are inevitable."

"That's the game in science," Rourke said. "If you observe enough, discover enough, you could predict anything; that is one of the most cherished Newtonian scientific beliefs. The Chaos Theory, made up of non-linear equations coupled with strange attractors and seemingly disjointed connections, throws it right out the window. Life will find a way. With your people, what is the normal life range?"

"It is much longer than yours; my people can expect to live between 750 and 900 of your years," The Keeper said. "While our journey was completed in 120 years of ship's time, within the life spans of some of the members of the fleet, you and I both know that 40,000 years passed on Earth."

Dr. Williams said, "Our 'sciences' are simple belief systems only a few hundred years old. As in medieval times, that science has started not to fit the world anymore; I fear we are approaching a not dissimilar situation to the one your people were dealt. Science has attained so much power that its practical limits begin to be apparent once again. Largely through science, the few millions of us live in one much smaller world, sparsely populated and with struggle with intercommunications."

"More than anything else, is it not also a question of how much 'knowledge' has been lost due to technology?" Rourke asked. "No human action is without consequence; as improvements are made, problems are discovered. An old Peace Corps volunteer once talked about the price of forgetting. He said, 'Often left behind are people who are shadows of what they once were and shadows of what we in the developed world are.'"

"He reported that at one older Catholic mission, for instance, nurses and missionaries have encountered patients brought in with burns or perforations of the lower intestine. Investigation revealed those afflicted had been treated for a variety of ailments with traditional medicines delivered in suppository form. The problem was not the medicines but the dosages. As the old healers died off, people would try to administer traditional medicines themselves or turn to healers who had only a partial understanding of what their elders knew."

The Keeper broke in, "John Thomas, the family of man has always consisted of many 'tribes.' The human family had many branches whose development was guided by environmental and ecological circumstances unique to different locations, but even with all of those circumstances, the creation of man was guided by our Creator. However, I cannot define how the Divine works."

"I do not understand the process; it is not mine to understand—it was His plan, and we are simply witnesses trying to interpret that which we see. Often, the 'evidence' is obscured by time, world changes, and circumstances we don't control. Why did my people develop the way we did? I don't know. Why was my civilization the first great one? I don't know that it was."

"I know your knowledge of the past is, at best, spotty. I have learned that you know about what you call Homo floresiensis, the Flores Man; there was also what you call, Homo habilis, Homo erectus, and over 10 other 'false starts' of what would eventually become Homo Sapiens who proceeded to colonize the continents, arriving in Eurasia 125,000 to 60,000 years ago, Australia around 40,000 years ago, and the Americas around 15,000 years ago."

"My point is that if all you know of your own history is based on a few finds scattered across the surface of this entire planet; if you still have ground to sift and oceans to explore—would you accept there may be more yet to be found and learned from?" The Keeper paused for effect, "As a point in hand, let me say that, before you, stands an example of... Shall we call us the Homo Atlantisian? We are a branch of the family of mankind your 'science' knew nothing about until our arrival. As the stones, bricks, and mortar of our civilization deteriorated or were hidden by time—what other missing pieces does the family of mankind still have that man has not yet discovered?"

Chapter Five

Tim Shaw was on his third cup of coffee when the Honolulu Chief of Police, Bryan Devlin, walked into Shaw's office, "Got a minute?" Devlin asked.

"Sure Chief, have a sit," Shaw motioned to an arm chair, while he stacked the files and reports he had been working on.

Devlin asked, "Tim, mind if I close the door? This isn't official."

Shaw leaned back in his chair as Devlin shut the door, poured a cup of coffee, and took a seat. "Whatcha got Chief?"

Devlin slid a file folder across to Shaw, "What do you know about this?"

Tim opened the file and did a quick scan, "I don't know anything about it. Where did you get this?"

The Chief said, "It came in this morning."

The file had a single letter in it from the Office of the Secret Service with a single line of type and a signature block. Captain Timothy Shaw was requested at the Office of the Director, U.S. Secret Service at 0900 hours, two days from now; signed by James A. Nixon, Director, Special Officers and Technical Division. Shaw shook his head, "Chief, I have no idea what this is about. I haven't had interaction with OSS since the brouhaha during Michael Rourke's inauguration."

"You're sure?"

"Absolutely, but I'll make the meeting and brief you as soon as I get out of it."

*****

Two days later, Jim Nixon, Director of the Special Officers and Technical Division, stuck his head out of his office and waved Shaw to come in. Dressed in a pressed suit, his appearance was much different from when he and his son were killing the Single Malt Scotch.

"Captain Shaw, pleasure to finally meet you," Nixon said.

"Director, what is this about?" Tim asked, setting his fedora on the floor next to his chair.

"Tim, may I call you Tim?" Shaw nodded his head. "We are in a bit of an issue right now. President Rourke called me into his office last Friday morning for a closed-door meeting. He is interested in making some changes in how the OSS operates; your name came up, and apparently President Rourke appears to know quite a lot about you."

Shaw nodded, "Director, I'm pretty sure you already know he is my daughter's brother-in-law, so just cut to the chase."

"Tim, with the current national and international situations this country is facing, the President wants some changes," Nixon explained. "Don't ask me what those changes are because neither he nor I have figured all of that out; here's what we are thinking about." Nixon handed Shaw a file.

"The President and I agree the simplest and most intelligent way is to proceed to create a new section within the OSS dedicated to a 'specific set of tasks.' The leader will report to me as the Director for Special Officer Positions. You must be a U.S. Citizen—which you are. You must be at least 21 years of age and younger than 40 at time of appointment—which you're not, but I can waive that requirement."

"You must have visual acuity to be correctable to 20/20 in each eye—which you do. You must pass a top secret clearance and undergo a complete background investigation, to include driving record check, drug screening, medical, and polygraph examinations—you have passed everything already but the drug test and polygraph examination—which you can take care of today—if that is acceptable."

"You are already familiar with all phases of protective responsibilities sufficient to assist in protective movements, cover designated security posts, and drive protective vehicles. You have proficiency in the use of various firearms, knowledge of arrest techniques and procedures, and your police training will be acceptable for what we need. I know you're coming up on retirement; that's in what, two months?"

Shaw nodded again.

"Okay," Nixon continued, "I am authorized to offer you the position of Chief of this new special project if you're interested. The position would start immediately, and your retirement will not be affected. Upon acceptance, if you do accept, the paperwork will be initiated to place you in a terminal leave status from the department, and your retirement will be moved forward with no loss in pay or benefits."

"Why me?" Shaw asked; he was starting to feel uncomfortable.

"I don't know," Nixon smiled a little sardonically. "What I am authorized to tell you is after a search of potential candidates, over 200 of them, your name came out second on the list, and number one had to go on medical leave over the weekend. Ergo, you are the man; seems like you were in the right place at the right time."

Shaw squirmed a bit and said, "First time that has ever happened. I have always subscribed to the thought by Steven Wright, 'When everything is coming your way, you're in the wrong lane.'"

Nixon nodded but pressed on, "Tim, there is only one problem. I need your decision now; the President was adamant the position has to be filled, and development of the Section and its implementation has to begin immediately. Here are the salaries and benefits package." He handed a sheet of paper to Shaw.

A low whistle was the only response. "Director, I need a little time here. I have to talk to my Chief before I do anything. How much time can I take?"

"Tim, I'll tell you honestly. If you are interested, I'll call and try to get your Chief over here within the hour. You can speak to him privately and give me your answer. If you accept, we have to do the drug test and polygraph test today. If you pass both, you start at 0700 tomorrow. If you want me to call your Chief, I'm placing you into a sequestered state. I need your cell phone, and you are to have no contact with anyone other than your Chief. What do you say?"

Shaw stood up and started pacing back in forth of the Director's desk; this was all coming too fast for him to process. Finally, he stopped, facing the Director. He pulled his cell phone out, handed it to the Director, and said, "Make the call."

By the time Shaw finally left the OSS, he had obtained not only the acqui-escence of Chief Devlin but his congratulations. Shaw gave Devlin his HPD credentials, keys, and a list of passwords. Devlin agreed to forward Nixon Shaw's file. Shaw had pissed in the bottle, plugged into the polygraph, and passed both. Seven hours after his arrival, very Special Agent in Charge, Timothy Shaw, walked back to his car with a new set of federal credentials and a new mission in life.

Nixon placed a call a call to the President, "Sir, just wanted to report it all went as planned. Everything is completed, and he starts tomorrow at 0700."

"Jim," Michael Rourke said, "I owe you one. Does he suspect this was any-thing other than legit?"

"Not a hint, and Mr. President, I personally think this is a brilliant idea. We can finally create a program that will work the way it is supposed to without all of the territoriality and interagency bickering."

"That's the plan, Jim. Thanks again." Rourke hung up and smiled at what he hoped would be the best kept Rourke secret of all times and dialed his dad's number.

"Okay, Dad, looks like everything is playing just like we wanted."

Chapter Six

Three hours later, Dr. William A. Sloan, the Geologic Anthropologist, John Rourke, and The Keeper were sitting in the Mid-Wake Research Institute's Linguistics Section's auditorium. Mid-Wake, the experimental underwater colony, had not only survived The Night of The War but expanded and thrived. It was from Mid-Wake that virtually all of the racial stock of the new United States had originated. As such, Mid-Wake had also positioned itself as the quazi-guardian of scientific knowledge and research.

Sloan, a short man wearing a white lab coat who, if he stretched, might make 5'6" said, "Paleontology is a science seeking to uncover the history of all life on Earth by examining multiple lines of evidence, including fossils and how they are formed and preserved, stratigraphy, biogeography, histology, chemistry, and Linguistics. Linguistics has shown me that paleo-humans communicated their stories and legends verbally through oral histories."

"The guardians of those oral histories were trained to pass those stories down generation to generation without change or interpretation. Around the 4th millennium BC, the businesses of trade and administration outgrew human memory, and writing became a more dependable method of recording and presenting transactions in a permanent form. There was also the political imperative of recording historical and environmental events."

"The ancient author H.G. Wells once said that 'Writing has the ability to put agreements, laws, and commandments on record. It made the growth of states larger than the old city states possible. It made a continuous historical consciousness possible. The command of the priest or king and his seal could go far beyond his sight and voice and could survive his death.'"

"Writing is the representation of language that uses a set of symbols. It is different from illustration, such as cave drawing and painting. Writing began as a reliable means for transmitting information, maintaining financial accounts, keeping historical records, and similar activities. In both ancient Egypt and Mesoamerica, writing may have evolved through the development of calendars, astronomical records, and a political necessity for recording historical and environmental events. The oldest known use of writing in China was in divination in the royal court."

"Historians draw a distinction between prehistory and history, with history defined by the advent of writing. The cave paintings and petroglyphs of prehistoric peoples can be considered precursors of writing but are not considered writing because they did not represent language directly. Language existed long before writing. As simple instinctive animals became more evolved mentally, they needed to communicate; they became sentient. Sentience is the ability to feel, where reason is the ability to think. Wisdom is also the comprehension of what is true coupled with optimum judgment as to action and abstract thought. This appeared to be unique to the genus Homo."

"The most significant benchmark or line of demarcation between our pre-human ancestors and early man was not tool-making. Several of our pre-human ancestors had tools; rather, I state it was the development of oral communication that allowed complex information, ideas, and concepts to be shared from one individual to another, or to a group."

The Keeper nodded and with a smile said, "As our two sciences began to be 'developed,' our two races must accept the fact there..." He paused, thinking of the correct words. "There are a myriad of alternatives or possibilities as to what became 'scientific information.' There are a number of roads or theories that will lead to the same result; look at the differences between your science and ours. Science is simply information, and with information, there are also several relevant questions such as: Who has it? Where do they keep it? How do we encourage them to share it? How is it created? Who else needs it? How is it communicated? How is it kept up-to-date? How and where is it stored? Which knowledge is relevant, now and in the future? How much is it collectively worth? Which is the most valuable? Is it used in the appropriate areas/situations? Is knowledge shared between dissimilar cultures to be applied in a different way which results in revolutionary improvements? What results can be created using existing knowledge? And lastly, where are areas of potential knowledge loss, and how can you mitigate that loss?"

"As for our own Dark Ages, that came when Rome fell," Rourke said. "Rome had kept things organized, with the paying of taxes and all, not the least of which were roads, a system of law, etc. Major settlements soon became abandoned. Science, especially medicine and architecture, astronomy, and all of the arts took giant steps backwards. The earth was flat, and hell was below the earth's crust and filled with fire, brimstone, witches, devils, and bad spirits. This is much different from the learned writings of Greek scholars."

The Keeper, agreeing, said, "Information is a commodity; knowledge is the manifestation of that information. It can be lost."

Chapter Seven

The U.S. Secret Service's Office of Research, Intelligence, and Operations, (ORIO) now headed by retired Honolulu Police Department Captain Tim Shaw was going to be unlike anything any law enforcement agency had ever had to play with. It was to be a Federal program that could act as a clearing house of information and intelligence gathering without the petty pissing contests between federal, state and county law enforcement agencies.

From an operational standpoint, that type of flexibility was also planned. ORIO had the ability and authority to "cherry pick" the best that law enforcement and the military had to offer and to combine them into a more effective unit. The only sticking point was there wasn't a lot of time to have it functional. By 0730 of his first duty day, Shaw was already running into obstacles. Shaw had thought he was going to be running the show; he didn't realize he *was* the show.

He went to Nixon's door and knocked by 0745; Nixon waved him in. "I've got a problem, Boss."

"What is it Tim?"

"You didn't tell me I was the Lone Ranger. Where are my Tontos?"

"Tontos? Are you saying you're the Chief and where are your braves?"

"Exactly."

Nixon, picked up his phone, punched several numbers, and said, "Bill, can you come down to my office?" A few minutes later, Bill Griffin, the head of Human Resources, arrived. "Bill, this is Tim Shaw; he's running that new project I spoke to you about." The two shook hands.

"Bill," Shaw said, "I need two things from you. I have to create a staff, and I need to know what authority I have to screen and hire folks."

"As I understand it, and correct me if I'm wrong Director, you're free to hire who you want and need. Of course, you have to decide their pay grades, and you have to stick to our standing guidelines," which he handed to Shaw. "And, they have to meet these qualifications," he said, handing Shaw another form.

"Outside of these restrictions, you can pretty well do what you want to do. By the way, this is the address of where your offices are. I have a man standing by there to give you a walkthrough of the building and explain security and things like that. I have also included my contact information if you need to get in touch with me in a hurry."

Shaw turned to the Director, "Do I have a vehicle, Boss?"

Nixon dialed another number, told someone to have a vehicle for Special Agent in Charge Shaw ready, then hung up and said, "It will be ready for you by the time you get to the motor pool."

"Where's the motor pool?"

"At the lowest level in the building, you need this access card." Taking the card, Shaw headed to the elevator. By the time he opened the door to his apartment, Special Agent in Charge Shaw had put in an 18-hour day and was bushed. Setting two alarm clocks, he chocked down a piece of pizza from the evening before and climbed in bed with his clothes still on. His plan was to shower in the morning, and it would wake him up.

*****

Shaw awoke with a start but just laid there. His arm had "fallen asleep" under him, tingling as he tried to move it, and he had to piss. It was all so familiar; the memories bubbled up from years past, washing over him and threatening to drown him with their intensity.

Earthquakes had been frequent then, volcanic ash routinely fell on Honolulu, and a rift was splitting the floor of the Pacific Ocean; that rift was going to destroy what was left of mankind and probably the planet, had it not been for Dr. Thorn Rolvaag successfully deploying nuclear warheads.

In the span of just a few days, the rift had been stopped and the planet was saved. Dr. Dietrich Zimmer had tried to kill humanity and failed, and Tim's son Eddie was shot during a SWAT operation. Patrol Officer Linda Cunningham had picked Shaw up at the hospital moments after the doctor's report; Eddie was going to make it. Mentally and physically exhausted, Shaw had accepted the ride home. Neither Tim nor Officer Cunningham had eaten, and he had asked Linda if she wanted a bite of supper.

It had been innocent enough; hell, she was two years younger than Emma, and Shaw had known her father for years; it was perfectly innocent. Linda had offered to cook for him in his apartment and then stayed the night. The next morning, his arm was asleep under Linda's head, which rested on his shoulder, and he had to piss. He figured when she woke up she would leave and that would be the end of it. In reality, it was the beginning.

For the next eight months, he had been happy coming home and finding her there, when her shift had allowed for it. Since his wife had died, Shaw had crawled deeper and deeper into his job. Linda dragged him kicking and scream-ing back to life. Maybe, he smiled; he hadn't kicked and screamed that much after all. Then, one night, just after New Year's, he got the call.

Linda had gotten the call of a Robbery in Progress at a convenience store about five blocks behind her. She executed a bootlegger turn, reversing her direction of travel, switching on her lights and siren, and running Code Three. At the third intersection she was passing through, she caught a green light and stomped the accelerator. She never saw the truck bust the red light.

The truck slammed into her driver's door. Though there was not a mark on her, the impact had snapped her neck. Linda Cunningham had died on impact, killed by a drunk teenage driver.

When Shaw rolled up on the scene, Linda looked like she was asleep. "At least she didn't suffer," was all Tim's partner Steve could think of to say.

"Bullshit," was all Shaw could think to say; he would suffer enough for the both of them. For the second time in his life, the fire in his belly went out. Since that night, Shaw went through the motions of living, not the experiences. He had been with no one else since that night and had vowed he would never be with anyone again. Tim Shaw's tough guy persona could not protect his heart, and he could not take loss well.

He did not subscribe to "it is better to have loved and lost than never to have loved at all;" the loss hurt too damn much. This morning, he looked at the alarm clock remembering. Finally, he rubbed his arm back to life and did the same thing he had done that morning so long ago. He wiped a tear from his eyes, got up, took a leak and a shower, and then went to work.

Chapter Eight

Shaw sat reading the plaque hanging on his office wall. The brass plate mounted on a cherry wood base was to the left of the door and faced his private desk. "The vision of the United States Secret Service is to uphold the tradition of excellence in its investigative and protective mission through a dedicated, highly-trained, diverse, partner-oriented workforce that employs progressive technology and promotes professionalism. The mission of the United States Secret Service is to safeguard the nation's financial infrastructure and payment systems to preserve the integrity of the economy and to protect national leaders, visiting heads of state and government, designated sites, and National Special Security Events."

Few "citizens" knew the Secret Service Division had actually been created on July 5, 1865 in Washington, D.C. to suppress counterfeit currency. Chief William P. Wood was sworn in by Secretary of the Treasury Hugh McCulloch. In 1894, the Secret Service began informal part-time protection of President Cleveland.

Following the assassination of President William McKinley in 1901, Congress directed the Secret Service to protect the President of the United States. Two operatives were assigned full-time to the White House. In 1908, the Secret Service began protecting the president-elect. Also, President Roosevelt transferred Secret Service agents to the Department of Justice. They formed the nucleus of what would later be the Federal Bureau of Investigation.

Permanent protection of the president began with statutory authorization to protect the president-elect in 1913. In 1951, Congress passed legislation that permanently authorized Secret Service protection of the president, his immediate family, the president-elect, and the vice president, if he wished it.

Protection remained a key mission of the United States Secret Service; the Secret Service would provide protection for the president, the vice president, other individuals next in order of succession to the Office of the President, the president-elect, the vice president-elect, and their immediate families. That protection extends to former presidents and their spouses, except when the spouse remarries for a period of not more than 10 years from the date the former president leaves office and their children of former presidents until age 16.

They also protect visiting heads of foreign states or governments and their spouses traveling with them, other distinguished foreign visitors to the United States, and official representatives of the United States performing special missions abroad. Within 120 days of a general presidential election, they protect "major" presidential and vice presidential candidates as well as their spouses.

As defined by statute, that means those individuals identified as such by the Secretary of Homeland Security after consultation with an advisory committee consisting of the Speaker of the House of Representatives, the minority leader of the House of Representatives, the majority and minority leaders of the Senate, and one additional member selected by the other members of the committee.

Up until a few days ago, the workings and mission of the OSS weren't particularly relevant to Shaw; then, he went to work for them and began to realize the system had a lot of complications and inefficiencies. However, making changes wasn't going to be easy; bureaucracies were like that. Tim Shaw was professional enough to realize that and street cop enough to know changes were needed. Telling somebody that "your baby's ugly, and your stuff is broken," however true, was not the way to ingratiate yourself to the bosses, particularly when you are the "new kid on the block."

Shaw had long accepted the adage that "your most favorable employee is the last one you hired. That person will ask one question no one else will, WHY?" Now, Shaw was the last one hired; his lack of indoctrination into "that's the way we've always done things" gave him a fresh perspective.

Chapter Nine

John Rourke knew the world had been different in 1952 when the Cold War was at its coldest and the House Un-American Activities Committee was looking for communists under beds. Newspaper accounts from that time covered the "discovery" of UFOs, and he had been privy to CIA records that showed him more. Few people knew it, but as far back as 1956, the U.S. Air Force had a couple of Cold War-era plans to build two round, vertical take-off and landing aircraft that could only have been described as "flying saucers." One disk-shaped craft was designed to reach a top speed of Mach 4 and reach a ceiling of over 100,000 feet. The Air Force had contracted the construction of the craft to a Canadian company, Avro Aircraft Limited in Ontario.

One report concluded that the flying saucer would work as designed. "It is concluded the stabilization and control of the aircraft in the manner proposed—the propulsive jets are used to control the aircraft—is feasible and the aircraft can be designed to have satisfactory handling through the whole flight range from ground cushion takeoff to supersonic flight at very high altitude," the report stated. "Additional tests to completely substantiate this performance are shown to be required," the report noted.

UFO sightings were being called in around the country on almost a daily basis up to and including Air Force pilots reported being chased by flying saucers. The sense of dread was turning to frenzy, and the CIA decided something had to be done.

The deputy head of the CIA's Office of Scientific Intelligence, H. Marshall Chadwell, and others in the CIA were fearful the Soviet Union was developing a secret weapon based on the "flying discs" that the Nazis had been developing in the last months of the Second World War. One of their engineers, 31-year-old John Frost, was studying the "Coanda effect," named after Henri-Marie Coanda, who had said that a turbojet would not only provide thrust by sucking in air, but it could also create a vacuum above the wing and thereby produce extra lift.

Frost's research was both dynamic and in almost total secrecy. His goal was to develop a vertical takeoff and landing VTOL craft; his company's management had been overjoyed when the first flights were moderately success-ful. The Public Relations Department designed brochures to capitalize on the aircraft's boundless potential as soon as the cloud of secrecy was removed. It would be called the Avrocar, and it would spawn a string of civilian and military spinoffs. There was even an Avrowagon on the drawing board for the family of the future. Plans were being drafted for an Avroangel, an air ambulance that would zip to the scene of an accident and land on the spot and an Avropelican for air-sea rescues and anti-submarine warfare. But alas, the Avrocar became dangerously unstable at heights over 2.5 meters and after an investment of $7.5 million; the Defense Department killed the Avrocar in 1961.

What had always concerned Rourke was where the original concepts had come from. It was, at least in John's mind, too radical a jump to write off as a result of "brilliant engineering and design." The questions raised by Roswell and the seemingly quantum leaps in technology were, for John Thomas Rourke, tied together a few years later and answered on a frozen field when he was sent to investigate the crash of an unidentified flying object and saw the craft's dead pilot.

Rourke had become convinced the technology Avro had been trying to per-fect had not originated on Earth any more than the Vertical Take Off and Landing technology the Nazis had been working on the last few years of World War Two. However, all of that remained speculation because Rourke had been forced to destroy the craft to prevent its technology from falling into the hands of the Russian KGB.

Chapter Ten

Tim Shaw was a pragmatic cynic; while he knew coincidences rarely had a place in police work, he also knew that they happened. He was also fond of quoting Steven Wright, an American comedian from before the Night of the War. He had discovered Wright going through John Rourke's cache of videos he had brought from his old Retreat.

Wright's deadpan delivery of ironic philosophical one-liners fit Shaw's personality. Wright was the guy who once said, "I woke up one morning, and all of my stuff had been stolen...and replaced by exact duplicates." Another of his sayings was, "Borrow money from pessimists; they don't expect to get it back." Shaw called them "Wrightisms."

Steven Drake, the senior attorney assigned to OSS, walked into Shaw's office unannounced, resplendent in a suit that had to cost $3,000 and began questioning him. "So," Drake said, "what are you doing?"

Shaw looked up from the mound of paperwork with a quizzical look, "And, who might you be?"

"I'm Drake, OSS' lead attorney," Drake said. Without an offer of a handshake, he sat down, not waiting for an invitation. "I want to know how much of a pain in my ass you're going to be."

Shaw sat there without a response.

"Let's get the ground rules established right now," Drake continued. "I have to review everything you do before you do it; got that? I don't need and won't tolerate some upstart mucking up the works here. And by the way, I have a photographic memory."

Shaw leaned back in his chair and took a sip of coffee and a deep breath; he didn't have time for this crap. "Okay Counselor, here is a Wrightism for you, '99% of lawyers give the rest a bad name.'"

"First of all, I don't report to you. Second, I don't report to you, and thirdly, I don't report to you. Now, here is how the Rules of Engagement are going to work with me. If you want to speak with me, call and make an appointment.

Provided an equally convenient time can be arranged, you may come to my office, or I'll be happy to come to yours. Otherwise, the answer will be no."

"If you have a problem with me, talk to me or talk to the Director. I'm sorry, but this meeting is now over. You will leave my office, or I will remove you. Here is yet another Wrightism for you, Sir, 'Everyone has a photographic memory; some just don't have film in the camera.' You have set the tenure of our relationship; I regret that because from this point forward, if everything seems to be going well, I will assume I've obviously overlooked something. Get out."

After a moment of intense stares, Drake stood, spun on his heel, and walked out slamming the door. Shaw took a sip of the cold coffee, looked around the office, and threw a Wrightism at the walls, "I'd kill for a Nobel Peace Prize."

Chapter Eleven

In her other life as Natalia Tiemerovna, a former Major in the Russian KGB, she had been surreptitiously adopted as a niece by General Ishmael Varakov after her real parents were killed by the KGB. After their deaths in a "road accident," Natalia trained as a KGB agent, reaching the rank of Major by the beginning of the war. Married to the unpredictable and often exceedingly ruthless Vladimir Karamatsov—the head of the KGB in America—whom she eventually left after being beaten and otherwise mistreated, she developed a close relationship with Rourke and his family. Natalia's favorite weapons were a silenced Walther pistol, an M-16, and a Bali-Song knife.

Today, as she often did, Natalia found herself thinking of her adopted uncle, Ishmael Varakov, an absolute warrior and the leader of the Soviet Occupation Forces in America. Varakov many times had also shown himself to be a patriotic, honorable, and reasonable Soviet soldier. He had, at times, helped John Thomas Rourke to stop some of the more extreme plans of the KGB.

Varakov was at his best spewing withering insults at one of his country's intelligence assets known as Randan Soames. Soames had survived the Night of the War to become a person of importance in the remnants of the U.S. Federal Government; Soames was, in fact, the Commander of Paramilitary Forces for Texas and one of Samuel Chambers' most trusted confidants.

Soames had been turned by the KGB who was blackmailing him because he was also a pedophile. Varakov had made it clear to Soames that, if he made the slightest error for any reason, Varakov would reveal him to the Americans. He also informed the man that, if he ever harmed another child and Varakov learned of it, Varakov would kill the spy by his own hand.

As it eventually turned out, John Thomas Rourke much later found himself capturing Soames. Rourke had the injured spy at gunpoint and promised him morphine with at least a limited chance for survival in exchange for the means to radio Varakov. Randan Soames' pain was incredible, and he agreed to the deal, providing a radio. Rourke, however, had lied to him; Soames' misdeeds could not be allowed to continue. As a perverted pedophile and a traitor to his own country, he had committed crimes both against nature and mankind. Rourke put an end to the story once and for all; he executed Soames both for his past crimes and in the name of final justice.

Varakov and John Rourke were hard men from different circumstances and different political systems, but Natalia had learned, in spite of their differences, she had loved both men; they were both heroic human beings. This lesson she had carried the rest of her life.

Natalia's world had changed so much since her old life, now married to Michael Rourke the President of the United States; Natalia Tiemerovna Rourke was finding a challenge where one had not been expected. This First Lady status was both far more involved than she had expected, but it was also somewhat unfocused, undisciplined, and ill-defined. The First Lady of the United States, called FLOTUS, first of all is supposed to be the hostess of the White House.

Her uncle had told her once, "If you're not living on the edge, you're taking up too much room." While the pageantry of her position was fascinating, the inactivity was choking for a person who thrived on activity and action. The night before, Natalia had read a report Michael had referred to him by the Department of Archeology and Antiquities. It dealt with a recent discovery at an older site that was now under reinvestigation.

Natalia, wearing a black casual outfit with her signature single-strand of natural pearls, found herself intrigued by the prospect of turning to the past in search of something to occupy her present—possibly even her future. She called Dr. William Sloan, the Geologic Anthropologist from Mid-Wake, with a question.

Sloan acknowledged, "Yes Ma'am, you are correct. There are some fascinating new discoveries at Göbekli Tepe in Turkey. I could send you a report and meet with you later today if you wish?" Natalia thanked Sloan and made an appointment to meet him at the White House after lunch.

The report arrived eight minutes later as an electronic transmission. It read:

The following core information was gathered from reports obtained from the Smithsonian Museum and other archaeological and religious reports dating back to the original discovery of Göbekli Tepe.

"Göbekli Tepe, which in Turkish means 'Potbelly Hill,' is a hot spot of archeological activity right now; it is located at latitude 37.476300 N and longitude 39.011000 E. NOTE: Göbekli Tepe is not far from the current northern glacial boundary."

"The site had first been identified in 1964 in a survey conducted by Istanbul University and the University of Chicago; the theory had been the hill could not entirely be a natural feature probably and was the location of a Byzantine cemetery that lay beneath the hill. Early digs had located a large number of flints and the presence of limestone slabs everyone thought were Byzantine grave markers. It had been a Neolithic hilltop sanctuary and is the oldest known human-made religious structure. The site had most likely been erected by hunter-gatherers in the 10th millennium BCE."

"Unfortunately, the hill had been under agricultural cultivation, and literally, generations of local farmers had moved rocks and slabs placing them in clearance piles. The damage done to archaeological evidence can only be described as 'impactful with much destroyed in the process.'"

"Early digs also began documenting the architectural remains of structures, and it was soon discovered there were T-shaped pillars facing southeast. Again, unfortunately many of these pillars had apparently undergone severe damage and destruction, presumably by the same farmers who had mistaken them for ordinary large rocks."

"The site contains 20 round structures which had been buried purposefully or at least by the sands of time. Only four had been excavated. With diameters ranging from between 30 and 100 feet, each is decorated with massive, mostly T-shaped limestone pillars that are the most striking feature of the site. These limestone slabs, it was reasoned, had been quarried from bedrock pits located around 330 feet from the hilltop, with Neolithic workers using flint points to carve the bedrock."

"One report states, 'The majority of flint tools found at the site are Byblos and Nemrik points. That Neolithic people with such primitive flint tools quarried, carved, transported uphill, and erected these massive pillars, astonishing the archaeological world, and must have required a staggering amount of manpower and labor.'"

"The location had been rediscovered only a few years ago. It had been literally lost in antiquity for centuries following the Night of the War. Over the last two years, coordinated digs had been restarted and with new technology had moved forward rapidly. The figures on the pillars unearthed so far represent animals of all shapes and class, a literal 'Noah's Ark.'"

"Interestingly, Göbekli Tepe is located in the shadow of Mount Ararat where Noah's Ark was said to have been left after The Flood. This leads to what we are now calling 'The Noah's Altar Theory.'"

"The Bible states that the very first thing Noah did when he safely landed was build an altar to God; Genesis 8:20 states, 'Then Noah built an altar to the LORD.'"

"It is possible that Göbekli Tepe could be Noah's Altar. This altar could be his work of praise to the Almighty God. What would such an altar look like? Wouldn't it probably have animals carved on it? Isn't Noah synonymous with animals?"

*****

Sloan arrived 15 minutes early for his meeting with Natalia. "Here is another 'strange' twist to the story," he said. "We have determined that not only had Göbekli Tepe been abandoned and lost to history millennia ago, but it was also purposely buried by tons of soil carefully packed around the structures until everything was invisible to the naked eye. It was so important to that culture; they wanted to save it from invading hordes or other destruction, even if that meant loss. Whatever their final reasoning, our ancient ancestors had, without even meaning to, actually carefully preserved this amazing archaeological site for us. Otherwise, like so many other locations not so preserved, it would eventually have been reduced to rubble, and we may never have seen it or known about it."

Natalia said, "As it is, it simply lay underground for millennia, undisturbed and intact?"

Sloan nodded, "You are correct."

"So," she said, "what it is and what it tells us about ancient man is nothing short of astounding."

"Exactly," Sloan said. "Göbekli Tepe was not constructed by 'people a stone's throw away from Cavemen.' The superior stone work and reliefs show that master stonemasons were at work here. One example of the carved pillars and monuments is decorated with human hands in what could be interpreted as a prayer gesture with a simple stole or surplice engraved above; this may be intended to signify a temple priest. Few humanoid figures have surfaced at Göbekli Tepe, but they include the engraving of a naked woman posed frontally in a crouched position similar to figures found in Neolithic North Africa. Some of the T-shaped pillars picture human arms which indicate they represent the bodies of stylized humans or anthropomorphic gods. But, this is what I wanted you to see."

He handed Natalia a single piece of paper. Zima continued, "Two days ago, I received a transmission from the team leader at Göbekli Tepe. Here is a photo and a new inscription just uncovered." Natalia sat stunned, unsure of what to say but knowing what she had to do.

"Here's another interesting part of the puzzle," Sloan continued. "When this report came out, I started digging. It is entirely too early to do anything but offer a hypothesis. I believe similar, if not the same inscription has been found before at other sites. However, due to degradation due to age, partial obliteration, or simply not realizing the significance; this symbol has been overlooked, not reported, or simply reclassified as idiomatic drawings no one understood."

Natalia said, "Dr. Sloan, you do not know this, but there was no record, at least in the Western world, of this image prior to the Night of the War that survived. In fact, there is only one person living who can testify it was ever seen prior to a few weeks ago. John Thomas Rourke saw this image on the buckle of an extraterrestrial pilot that had been killed in the crash of his UFO ship several years before the Night of the War. Records that survived from the U.S. don't mention it, and no other governments have acknowledged any reports on their side. However, I know of one other government that had and, therefore, probably still has a record of this image. I saw this in the archives of the Union of Soviet Socialist Republics. I know for a fact that Russia still retains those archives and has knowledge of this image. Where else do you think it has been found?"

Sloan said, "I don't know, but I have started a search."

"Dr. Sloan," Natalia said, "this may tie into something really sinister and may answer some very serious questions. This is something I want to coordinate with you. When could you mount an expedition to the area with an archaeological team?"

"I don't know if another expedition is even possible because of the political situations right now," Sloan said. "It may be easier to secure an expansion of the current one."

"Work your end and find out," Natalia said. "I have some things to do on my end before we lock anything in. Make sure your people are volunteers; I've got a hunch we will be moving into harm's way on this one."

Chapter Twelve

Michael Rourke, after the morning security briefings and now dressed in a Marine flight suit for a photo op, was headed to the Kaneohe Marine Air Base. He was scheduled to arrive at 2:00 p.m. Three heavy armored black SUVs negotiated Honolulu noontime traffic before heading east out of town.

Michael, in the second vehicle, was receiving a briefing from the head of his security detail when a green energy blast flashed from a hidden source and vaporized the right front quarter panel of the lead vehicle. The blast alone was sufficient to slam the vehicle a dozen feet to the left causing it to careen through the guardrail and down the steep incline. It was a miracle the vehicle did not roll over.

The official report would state, "The passenger in the right front passenger seat had died as a result of the greenish energy bolt's impact. The driver and the two agents in the back seat were slammed violently to the left, and the side air bags deployed. Those in the back seat were knocked unconscious. The vehicle's front end collided with a tree in the exact dead center of the hood. The impact crumpled the remainder of the front end beyond recognition. While the puncture proof gas tanks held, gas line connections to the vehicle's motor ripped loose, and the smell of gasoline permeated the vehicle. It took only seconds for ignition."

Michael's driver instinctively jammed the accelerator to the floor, and the heavy vehicle lunged forward; Rourke himself was shoved rather unceremoniously to the floor in the back seat. The third vehicle slowed only momentarily as it passed the gap in the guardrail before accelerating to close on the President.

The first radio communications simply said, "Attack, attack, attack... POTUS is under attack on Highway 63 headed east toward Kaneohe Marine Air Base. We are three miles into the Ko'olau Mountain Range. One vehicle disabled, unknown causalities. Scramble alert force, over." No sooner had that gone out than all of the radio frequencies used by the convoy were jammed by an unknown source, and contact with the convoy was lost.

Chapter Thirteen

John Thomas had recently established a ritual of sipping coffee on the patio and watching the blue ocean waves rolling, breaking, and spewing a white cloud as they crashed. It had become one of his favorite pastimes, and sharing these times with Emma had become a comfortable peaceful habit.

When Emma refilled his cup from the stainless carafe, it broke his silent reverie. Rourke looked up and smiled, "Emma, we humans don't have any surviving records of the Great War between the KI and the aliens or, for that matter, of the KI themselves. All traces of the KI's advanced civilization simply disappeared with the passing of time. Survivors of that last great battle were probably etched in history simply as the basis for our legends."

"Mankind, who was just emerging, was almost totally destroyed, and the rest of humanity were just learning the use of stone tools, clothing themselves in animal skins, and seeking shelter in caves. The few KI who survived here after the battle obviously retained the possessed knowledge of their destroyed civilization's wisdom, passing tantalizing bits and pieces of knowledge, at least for a few generations. Their tales of great exploits down through the ages appear as legend, myth, and alchemy."

Emma asked, "What was the war about, do we even know?"

"The Keeper told me," John nodded seriously. "Are you ready for this? It's about chlorophyll—that green pigment found in algae and plants. It is an extremely important biomolecule, critical in photosynthesis, which allows plants to absorb energy from light."

"On this planet, chlorophyll is everywhere. Every plant uses it; it is abundant here on this planet, but apparently it is a rare, very rare, commodity elsewhere. Evidently, it is essential for the alien race; apparently, they have evolved to the point that food, as you and I think of food, is irrelevant to them. Chlorophyll, however, is an essential part of their dietary needs; it allows for them to break down other compounds that keep them alive."

The Keeper said, "The KI offered to share Earth's chlorophyll with them, but coexistence was not the alien's plan; they wanted to dominate mankind and reduce humans to virtual slaves who functioned totally at their 'new master's' direction. The KI did not like slavery as an acceptable option. As it turned out, the alien force was driven away by the same global catastrophes they were escaping."

"Coincidently, the KI had already been preparing for a series of other types of disaster. Their scientists had been warning for generations the planet was approaching a series of natural events that would have catastrophic results for the KI civilization. Great geological upheavals were expected along with probable shifts of the magnetic poles and climatic changes that would affect all life on the planet. The KI evacuation was interrupted when the enemy appeared without warning."

She asked, "That's where you believe our 'legends' came from, those that remained?"

"Yes," he said. "Emma, here is the rest of the problem. Now that the KI have returned, at least according to The Keeper, many of the KI consider that the Earth was theirs, and they wish to reclaim it. They have no wish to destroy humanity, but there are elements within the KI that are far from benevolent. They consider the Earth to be their inheritance and view modern man as interlopers, little more than what you would call squatters. They remember our ancestors as primitive, and there exists certain... biases against all things that are not KI."

John's cell phone jingled unexpectedly; Rourke looked at the screen before saying to Emma, "Strange that Michael would be calling this early." Answering, Rourke said, "Good morning Michael..." Rourke listened for a moment before straightening in his chair. Slowly, his eyes hardened, and he asked, "How long ago?"

Emma could see that concern was now etched in John's face. "What's wrong?" she asked.

Rourke ignored her, staying focused on what was being said on the other end of the phone, "Any contact with the convoy?" Then, he said, "How soon?" followed by "I understand; keep me posted please," before closing the phone and standing and turning toward the ocean. Unconsciously, he pulled the double Alessi holster rig from the table and slipped it and the twin CombatMasters on; he shrugged his shoulders, settling the rig into its proper position. He slowly lit one of his black cigars. When it was going to his satisfaction, he flipped the Zippo shut and turned to Emma.

"Michael's in trouble. His convoy was hit while they were enroute to the Kaneohe Marine Air Base." Emma's hand flew to her mouth.

"All contact has been lost with his team; that's all we know right now. We have no idea about casualties." Taking another draw on the cigar, he said through clenched teeth, "The fear is it's a hit on Michael which could mean a hit on the entire Rourke clan, so the Secret Service has security details dispatched to cover us."

"When they get here, I want you to follow their instructions closely. I'm taking one of them with me to the site of the attack. I need you to contact the rest of the family and advise them."

"Do you want me to call Sarah?"

Rourke shook his head. "Not yet. We need more information; let's hold off until we have more facts." The screeching of tires out front announced the Secret Service's arrival, "Make sure we have all of the kids accounted for and keep them safe," Rourke said and turned, pausing just long enough to again settle the double Alessi holster rig in place and throw on his brown leather bomber jacket. Then, he left.

Chapter Fourteen

The smoke was now billowing around the crumpled SUV. Michael Rourke's vehicle and the remaining security vehicle were accelerating around the curves. Radio communications were being jammed; they had only gotten one message out. It seemed they had slipped the ambush and were now racing at breakneck speed toward the air base after crossing the Pearl Bridge just south of Mount Puu Keahiakahoa's 838 meter peak.

Rourke's driver, Hank Johnson, signaled for the trailing vehicle to pull alongside. They needed to communicate and get a plan; slowing to 50 and shouting over the wind and road noise, Johnson told the other driver to "Take the lead and clear the road ahead of us. Run Code Three to the air base. Keep trying to make contact, and let someone know where we are."

The second driver nodded, flashed the "thumbs up" sign, and accelerated to take the lead. Ten seconds later, a fusillade of energy blasts hit both SUVs; this second stage of the ambush lasted five seconds but had effectively destroyed both vehicles and apparently all passengers.

Chapter Fifteen

Vice President, Jason Darkwater, was just returning from Mid-Wake when he received the first notice of the attack moments before he landed in the capital. With President Rourke unaccounted for and possibly captured or dead, the Vice President found himself in a most unusual situation; he could not tell whether or not he was now the President.

Arriving at the Capital, Darkwater was ushered to the Situation Room where Jim Nixon, Director of the Secret Service Special Officers and Technical Division, was in intense conversation with Tim Shaw, Director of The U.S. Secret Service's Office of Research, Intelligence, and Operations. Representatives from the military, Emergency Services, law enforcement and every investigative agency in the government were clustered around live feed big screens trying to determine what had happened, how it had happened, and where the hell the President was.

Darkwater cleared his throat; the gathering grew quiet. "Ladies and Gentlemen, our primary focus right now is to locate President Rourke, determine his status, and bring this threat to an immediate and conclusive end. I want everyone cooperating; we can't afford the normal interagency bureaucracy. I want the Press Secretary to prepare a news release for immediate dissemination to the media. I want it truthful but guarded; we don't know yet what we're dealing with. I want the Speaker of the House and the Chief Justice brought here immediately; we're going to have to get ahead of these circumstances, and we have to do it now. Now, who can tell me what happened?"

Jim Nixon spoke first, "First of all Mr. Vice President, we're still trying to determine that. What I do know right now is that President Rourke and his protection detail were in a three vehicle convoy on their way to the Kaneohe Marine Air Base to welcome the fleet home from deployment when they came under attack by unknown forces. The lead vehicle was hit by an energy weapon and blasted off the highway. Of the six Secret Service personnel in that vehicle, two died."

"Agent Derrick Daniels was killed by the initial blast, and Agent Frank Wilson, the driver, was killed on impact. Wilson was able to keep the vehicle upright but not from impacting a tree after leaving the road. The other personnel have a variety of serious injuries, but at this time, they are expected to recover."

The Vice President said, "What about President Rourke?"

"Sir, we just don't know," Nixon said. "The second vehicle containing the President and the trailing vehicle both escaped the kill zone. We have aerial and ground searches in place and are monitoring all radio frequencies in the area. Unfortunately Sir, we just don't know yet. We have protection details dispatched to all senior leaders as well as the members of the Rourke family."

*****

Special Supervisory Agent in Charge John Anders, commander of the Secret Service's Special Response Unit, said, "Satellite surveillance is being blocked. We know roughly where the attack took place, and air craft have been dispatched; two jet fighters and four combat helicopters are enroute from the Marine Air Base. The jets should be over the area..." Anders checked his watch, "right now. Copters should be there in another 10 minutes, then we'll have some eyes in the sky. Additional ground troops are also enroute and should be on station shortly."

Anders, 42 years old, red-headed and wiry, stood in front of his team leaders. The OSS Special Response Unit members were seasoned veterans with specialized training and weaponry; in the vernacular of the "business," they were "high-speed, low drag." Broken into three nine-man teams, they had launched from Honolulu at the first report of the attack. Their armored all-terrain vehicles, well-known as AATVs, were equipped with the latest armament and communications gear; the members themselves were dedicated and focused. The mission was simple, locate and recover the President of the United States.

*****

Robert Johns, the Chief Justice of the Supreme Court, shook his head. "Mr. Vice President, right now we simply don't have enough information to proceed. Let me explain, Article I, Section 3, of the Constitution says, 'The Vice President of the United States shall be President of the Senate but shall have no vote unless they be equally divided. The Senate shall choose their other officers and also a President pro tempore in the absence of the Vice President or when he shall exercise the office of President of the United States.'"

"Article II, Section 1, of the United States Constitution provides that, 'In case of the removal of the President from office, or of his death, resignation, or inability to discharge the powers and duties of the said office, the same shall devolve on the Vice President ... until the disability be removed or a President elected.'"

"The 25th Amendment establishes procedures both for filling a vacancy in the office of the President and, subsequently, the Vice President as well as responding to Presidential disabilities. Here are the specifics: Section 1 says that 'in case of the removal of the President from office or of his death or resignation, the Vice President shall become President. Section 2 deals with similar situation for the Vice President; whenever there is a vacancy in the office of the Vice President, the President shall nominate a Vice President who shall take office upon confirmation by a majority vote of both Houses of Congress.'"

"Section 3 says that 'whenever the President transmits to the President pro tempore of the Senate and the Speaker of the House of Representatives his written declaration that he is unable to discharge the powers and duties of his office, and until he transmits to them a written declaration to the contrary, such powers and duties shall be discharged by the Vice President as Acting President.'"

"Section 4 does say, 'Whenever the Vice President and a majority of either the principal officers of the executive departments or of such other body as Congress may by law provide, transmit to the President pro tempore of the

Senate and the Speaker of the House of Representatives their written declaration that the President is unable to discharge the powers and duties of his office, the Vice President shall immediately assume the powers and duties of the office as Acting President.' We're not there yet."

"The other provisions state, 'Thereafter, when the President transmits to the President pro tempore of the Senate and the Speaker of the House of Representatives his written declaration that no inability exists, he shall resume the powers and duties of his office unless the Vice President and a majority of either the principal officers of the executive department or of such other body as Congress may by law provide, transmit within four days to the President pro tempore of the Senate and the Speaker of the House of Representatives their written declaration that the President is unable to discharge the powers and duties of his office. Thereupon, Congress shall decide the issue, assembling within 48 hours for that purpose if not in session.'"

"Finally, 'If the Congress, within 21 days after receipt of the latter written declaration, or if Congress is not in session, within 21 days after Congress is required to assemble, determines by two-thirds vote of both Houses that the President is unable to discharge the powers and duties of his office, the Vice President shall continue to discharge the same as Acting President; otherwise, the President shall resume the powers and duties of his office.'"

Closing the manila folder that carried his reference documents, Johns continued, "Right now, we do not know the President's status. I feel it is premature to take any action other than identify you as the 'Acting President.'"

Chapter Sixteen

Before the "Fight in the Forest," Randall Walls, the Emergency Management Services Director, had shared some "disturbances" he had found in aerial surveillance photos with Paul Rubenstein. These ultimately led to the discovery of the location of the secret infiltration of Captain Dodd's forces. Paul had been the first to understand the pattern which otherwise would have been unnoticed; once the pattern had been realized, they were obvious. This fact had never been released to the media.

After the attack on the day of Michael Rourke's inauguration, Paul had contacted Walls, and they had begun investigating aerial surveillance footage of the Honolulu area. Walls and Rubenstein were now pouring over the data, and they knew what to look for.

"You were right Paul," Walls said excitedly. "Here they are just like the last time but in a different area. They start only 10 days before the last attack. Here, day one, several of these visual disturbances occurred. This time, they are coming from several directions but always ending up here."

"I see it Randall," Rubenstein confirmed and pulled a topographic map from the bookshelf, spreading it on the table. "I have to make a phone call."

The call was answered simply, "Shaw."

"Tim, Paul Rubenstein here. I've got some information for you."

"Paul, I can't talk right now. We're a little busy."

"Tim, this is important. I think we may have located Michael." Tim Shaw sat up in his chair.

"Paul, this line is not secure." Shaw sat and motioned to one of his men to start a trace. "Give me a minute."

The Agent scribbled a note and handed it to Shaw, "Okay, I'll be there in 10 minutes. Paul, are you sure about this?"

"No Tim, but I think it is a pretty solid lead."

"I'm on my way." Shaw hung up the phone and turned to the other agents, "I want a secure SAT phone and three of you downstairs right now. Get me Director Nixon."

*****

Paul and Walls were briefing Shaw; Paul moved to the map, "This is the Waiāhole Forest Reserve area, north of Honolulu. Based on the data, we have a site identified. It appears there is an underground tunnel complex that dates back to the mid-twentieth century."

"My guess is that this site was prepped before the attack on the day of the inauguration," Walls said. "Probably, it is protected by the counter-illuminated camouflage technology we have seen before. Most likely, there is an invisibility cloak or a force field that assumes the colors and textures of its surroundings."

Shaw asked, "How big is this place?"

Paul referred to his notes, "This northern leg of the complex is 2.76 miles long and about 750 feet above sea level, connecting with side tunnels that come in from different directions and, specifically, the Kahana, Waikane, Waianu, and Waiāhole valleys. Our data shows there is an old railroad track inside the complex that was used to facilitate movement of personnel and equipment when the system was constructed."

"So we have six potential entry points." Shaw said.

Paul nodded, "Could be more but that's what we can see."

"You have the surveillance tapes?" Shaw asked.

Walls pulled the keyboard closer and hit several keys. "Like with the days just before the "Fight in the Forest," this activity went unnoticed. Here, 10 days before the attack, disturbances were always moving in the same direction, from the same direction, and ending right here. Day two—the same disturbances, but now from two directions all ending in the same place. Day three—more disturbances, multiple directions all ending here," he pointed toward the screen.

"You're sure these are real?"

"Tim," Paul said with emphasis. "These are the same patterns we saw that lead to the last battle. Randall has double-checked the satellite feeds and ran diagnostics as well as wind patterns, thermal atmospheric shifts, weather patterns, and bird migrations. There is something there. Now..." Paul nodded, and Walls brought up another satellite image.

Walls said, "This is the day of the attack on the inauguration; watch right here."

Moments before the attack, a "disturbance" could be seen over the Waiāhole Forest area and tracked southward. The disturbance, which looked to Shaw like a large puddle of water, was moving over the forest. You can still see the trees below but not as clearly as the trees not under the puddle. Suddenly just outside the city, the "puddle" disappeared. Then, four flying craft took its place, and the attack commenced.

This was Shaw's first aerial view of the attack, and though it did not last long, the attack's devastation was brought back with horrifying detail.

"Now, watch right here..." Rubenstein directed. One of the flying craft entered a plume of smoke coming from the crash scene of the passenger liner, but it never appeared on the other side. In its place, now that he knew what to watch for, Shaw found the "disturbance" and watched its path back to the Waiāhole Forest.

Walls pushed some more keys and the view changed, "This is Highway 63 where the first ambush was sprung yesterday."

It revealed three black SUVs on a convoy when a "disturbance" could be seen approaching from the north. It accelerated, passed behind the convoy, and moved ahead of it. Suddenly, the flying craft appeared for just an instant, and the lead vehicle was blasted off the road; just as quickly, the craft disappeared. Less than a minute later, it reappeared and attacked the remaining vehicles.

"Son of a bitch," Shaw said quietly.

"But watch, this is the important part," Paul said.

Again, viewing the screen, they noticed that immediately following the attack the craft disappeared again and the "disturbance" could be seen moving off to the north. Barely visible through the smoke of the burning vehicles, movement could be detected but not discerned. It appeared as though someone had survived the devastating attack.

"Why didn't my people find this?" Shaw asked with an edge to his voice.

"Well, Tim," Paul said. "They didn't know what to look for."

*****

Jason Darkwater had first met the Rourkes during an operation at Eden City, but he had not been the first in his family line to fight alongside the Rourkes. As Captain Darkwater then, he had never been a desk jockey and had participated in a number of military operations with the Rourkes. He was tough, dedicated, and a fighter when required, but he was also a thinker; he knew tactics because he had employed them. He had no fear of getting in harm's way himself; he also knew it took greater courage to send someone else into harm's way than going himself.

Darkwater had retired from the Navy as a Rear Admiral; less than one percent of career officers are promoted to flag rank. Darkwater graduated second in his class of over 900 midshipmen at the United States Naval Academy with a bachelor's degree in American political systems.

He had spent the majority of his time with the Office of Naval Intelligence. It is the leading provider of maritime intelligence to the U.S. Navy and joint war fighting forces as well as national decision makers and other consumers in the Intelligence Community.

Darkwater, born in Dallas, Texas, had attended John F. Kennedy High School where his mother worked as a math teacher. Darkwater was deeply inspired by his parent's attention to detail and "never quit" attitude. Darkwater's grandfather and father had both graduated from the U.S. Naval Academy and fought for the U.S in sea and air battles decades ago, each rising to the rank of Captain. Jason had followed their tradition.

Darkwater was accepted into the U.S. Naval Academy immediately after graduating high school. Following his graduation and commissioning, his flair for intelligence work finally had totaled up more operations than the next five other operatives. Between field assignments, he had served at each of the ONI subordinate centers in a variety of positions, eventually commanding the Kennedy Irregular Warfare Center.

With the appointment of a new Navy Chief of Staff however, the controversy started, and Darkwater was eventually being administratively removed from that position. It was reported he had "ruffled feathers" and conflicted with the Secretary of Defense—who later resigned—because Darkwater "wouldn't kiss his ass." In one investigative report, Chief of Naval Operations stated that, *"... People can say what they want to say, but Darkwater challenged people who did not want to be challenged. The guy is courageous, a patriot's patriot."*

Forced out by those he had challenged, Darkwater retired from the Navy that year to help care for his son who had been diagnosed with a severe genetic disorder. He retired as a one-star or Rear Admiral, as he did not hold the rank of two-star Admiral long enough to retain it as a permanent rank; as a final insult, his son had not survived.

In the vacuum left by the death of his son and his retirement, Darkwater realized he had to get a "game" or he'd lose his mind. Typically untypical, the apolitical Darkwater turned to politics. Many wondered, "How can a man who hated the politics of power decide that the best place to combat those politics was from the inside?" Even Darkwater had never found a satisfactory answer to that question.

Chapter Seventeen

Alpha Team of the Special Response Unit formed into three wedge-shaped lines across Highway 63; its job was to run the point and break trail for the other teams. The other two teams, laid out similarly, were positioned to follow Team One at a distance of one-quarter mile. Bravo Team's mission would be to drop out, isolate the attack scene, locate survivors, and determine as much as possible from the evidence available. Charley Team was to back up Alpha Team as necessary in its hunt for the President.

Anders and the Command Team would attempt to break whatever was causing the communications blackout, direct forces as needed, and arrange for evacuation and recovery of any survivors. He gave the signal, and the AATVs gunned their engines and roared down the highway, hopefully moving toward the watchful eye of Marine fighter jet air cover. Each AATV held a driver who was also responsible for communications, a turret gunner, and a heavy machine gunner.

Anders' vehicle, also armored, was larger; it contained a four-man team consisting of a driver, a weapon's specialist who manned the two heavy plasma cannons, a gunner who operated the twin heavy machine guns, and Anders who was in touch with Central Command and trying to clear the jamming situation. He was close enough now to see the smoke rising from the ambush site; several miles ahead, he thought he could see more smoke on the horizon.

Alpha Team blasted past the site without slowing. Bravo Team established security over watches with two squads, and the third charged through the destroyed guardrail and down the embankment. Charlie Team accelerated and closed on Alpha's rear. Anders' vehicle slowed as it passed the ambush site in the event they had to back up Team Two. Anders, call sign TACTICAL, keyed his microphone, "TACTICAL to Bravo; status, over."

"Bravo here, no sign of POTUS, TACTICAL. We have one KIA from the POTUS convoy, two in critical condition, who will require immediate dust off, medical evacuation and one with non-life threatening injuries. It appears to have been a heavy energy weapon blast that impacted the right front of the lead vehicle and blew it off the road and down the embankment. Security team is out but negative signs of the bad guys. Survivor says that, after they were hit, the other two vehicles followed procedure and attempted to leave the kill zone, over."

"Roger, Bravo," Anders said and rekeyed his mic. "TACTICAL to Alpha Team, over."

"Alpha, negative on POTUS, TACTICAL. I am closing on what looks to be a second ambush site. Heavy smoke is coming from what appears to be two closely located sources. Approximately one minute to scene, negative contact with opposing forces, yet, over."

"Alpha, any contact with friendlies? Over."

"Affirmative, we have air cover. Approaching scene, give me a minute. TACTICAL, we have located the other two vehicles, still zero contact with POTUS. Securing scene, we have two missing, four KIAs but again, no sign of POTUS. We're going to need aerial surveillance to scout the area, terrain not friendly to the AATVs, over."

Anders ordered his command vehicle to the side of the road; this would be his command post location. Changing frequencies, he contacted Central Command, "TACTICAL to Command, over." There was no answer; he tried twice more before making contact.

"TACTICAL, this is Command. Status, over."

"Command, this is TACTICAL. POTUS contact is negative. All three vehicles were destroyed; we have casualties at the first site and are awaiting a casualty report from the second site. We have two needing immediate dust off at the first site and two missing from the second site, including POTUS, over."

Anders got a signal from his driver; Team Three was trying to raise him on the tactical frequency. "Standby Command."

Switching channels, Anders said, "Charlie Team, this is TACTICAL, over."

"TACTICAL, this is Charlie. Alpha has secured the scene with two squads; Charlie Team supplemented by one of the squads from Alpha is expanding the search area. We have three KIA, one expectant; he probably would not survive even with medical help. One needs immediate evacuation, and there are two MIA including POTUS. There has been zero enemy contact, over."

Anders wiped his face with one hand, "Roger, Charlie. Have the choppers arrived? Over."

"Affirmative, TACTICAL just got here, over."

"Affirmative Charlie, we need a joint ground and air operational search pattern working, and we need it now, over." Switching frequencies, Anders gave the report to Central Command. The only response was, "Roger, out."

*****

Michael Rourke woke up slowly; consciousness was shimmering like the surface of a lake, and he was trying to swim up to it. He was down deep, a long way off, and his chest hurt; he didn't know if he would make it before he had to breathe in the water that would drown him.

Suddenly, his lungs filled, not with water but with life-giving air. He was leaning against a tree, his head hurt, and there was blood obscuring one side of his face. Sitting across from him with his eyes closed was Ken Farris, one of his protection team. Farris was hurt. A piece of metal protruded from his side, and he was in obvious discomfort in his abdominal area.

Nudging Farris' foot, Michael asked, "Ken, are you alright?"

Farris opened his eyes and smiled, "Hello, Mr. President. You had me worried, didn't know if you would wake up or not. That cut looks pretty bad."

Michael smiled, "Looks worse than it feels, how about you? Did any of the others make it?"

Farris shook his head, "Don't know, maybe Franklin, but I couldn't be sure. You were out cold, and the rest were either unconscious or dead. I had to get you outta there. I think we're safe here for a little while; the cover of smoke gave us a good screen to get away in. Haven't heard any sign of them following us. We're about a mile from the scene of the attack."

Rourke nodded, "What about you Ken? You carried me the whole way?"

Farris shook his head and with a grin said, "No Boss, I had to drag you the last quarter mile. You're a big boy."

Michael crawled over to Farris, "Thank you Ken. What can I do for you? You're hurting pretty badly."

"Don't think there is anything you can do," Farris said. "I'm not sure if it is the spleen or the liver, could be both I guess. Probably would make it if I could get to a trauma center, but I'm bleeding internally, and I'm getting weaker by the minute." Farris had diagnosed his injuries as matter-of-factly as if he were reading the Sunday paper. "Either the spleen or liver can be dangerous; if the damage was massive, I'd already have bled out. My radio and your cell phone are gone. Yes Sir, I searched you for it as soon as we were out of the danger zone; both are probably in the burning wreck. We can't contact anyone. Now Mr. President, I need you to listen to me. You need to get out of here, and you are not going to be able to haul me with you."

Michael frowned, "I'm not leaving you, not after you saved me. I'm not doing it." Farris leaned forward and grabbed Michael's shirt, "Yes, you are Sir, and you're going to do it right now. My job is to protect you, not the other way around."

Michael stood up and raised Farris to his feet, "I'm not leaving you behind my friend." Rourke threw Farris' arm around his own neck and took two steps before Farris collapsed and drug both of them to the ground.

Farris looked around and then said, "Yes, you are Boss. You have to hold out until our people can get here. It shouldn't take too awfully long, but you're alone, unarmed, and people are after you and I'm..." Before he could finish his thought, Secret Service Agent Kenneth Farris grimaced once, closed his eyes, and died.

Chapter Eighteen

Michael left Farris where he lie, checking for anything Ken Farris might have on him that he could use; he found nothing. Rourke stood, located the sun's position, and held his Rolex watch horizontally, pointing the hour hand at the sun. Noting the direction that lies exactly midway between the hour hand and the numeral 12 gave him south. While it was late morning, it was still morning; the sun was in the east. He started off at a trot, reasoning heading east would take him further from the site of the attack and closer to a search team he knew would be dispatched from the Marine Air Base.

His head hurt like hell, and the wound had started bleeding again. But, it was more like seepage than bleeding. *Well, this is a fine mess you've gotten yourself in*, Michael thought. He had the clothes he was wearing, and that was about it. He searched his surroundings for something, anything he could use for a weapon; he found nothing. He could use a large stick as a club or a large rock, but that meant closing with the killer; that simply was not an option. If Rourke could kill or incapacitate the killer, it would have to be from a distance. He ran, walked, and trotted for two hours before he rested.

Michael had been going to the air base for a photo opportunity to show his support for the military. He had been offered a ride in the back seat of one of the base's jets, courtesy of the unit commander. The Public Affairs Officer had suggested Michael be in a flight suit for the ride. "Trust me Sir, gonna make a hell of a shot." Going unarmed had not seemed to be a problem; after all, he was going to a Marine Base.

Now, he assessed his situation. His flight jacket was gone, probably just a smoldering blob somewhere in the vehicle. The Nomex flight suit had offered him protection from the vehicle fire, and the flight boots were giving him good ankle stability on his escape after Farris' death. He had his wrist watch, billfold, and A.G. Russell Sting 1-A, a copy of his father's famous knife; but, that was it.

Catching his breath and assessing his options, he realized he didn't have any. He was on foot with no weapons, no food, and no supplies. It was then from the depths of his memory it came slowly bubbling to the surface. He thought of his dad's old friend Jerry. Before the Night of the War, Jerry, a prolific writer and survival expert, had shown John what he called the Arrow. It was simple, easy to construct; John had taught young Michael how to make them as a child.

"Jerry told me it really wasn't his invention," his dad had said. "It has been known by a lot of names: the Swiss arrow, Dutch arrow, Yorkshire arrow, and even the Gypsy arrow. Originally, it was designed for war and hunting in areas that had not developed the bow yet. Like the Atlatl or throwing stick, it probably goes back 40,000 years. The arrow shaft is made from wood; green garden canes are perfect for the job, being straight and lightweight."

"A slit is cut at one end for the fletching. You could use a pair of playing cards or even cardboard. At the other end, you put a point. The important part is a notch is cut into the shaft, just below the flights or fletching. After the flights are inserted, the open end of the slit is closed with string or a rubber band to prevent the flights from falling out. To launch the arrow, the thrower uses a length of string that is longer than the length of the arrow itself."

"A knot is tied in one end of the string, and this is placed into the notch in the arrow shaft. The rest of the string is then passed around the shaft once and is made to align over and above the knot before being stretched down to the point end of the arrow. You keep the string tight and make sure the knotted end stays within the notch. You wrap the surplus around your throwing hand and grip the arrow near the point end of the arrow."

"The arrow is then held behind the thrower; make sure to keep the string taut. When you throw it, the throwing arm should be as fully extended. The arrow is thrown like a javelin but held much closer to the tip. Following through with the throwing hand allows the string to provide additional forward force on the arrow, extending the length and reach of the thrower's arm in a fashion similar to a sling. A considerable distance can be achieved, easily twice as far as you could throw the arrow without the string."

His dad had told him that kids usually used pieces of cane for the arrow shafts since they were round and smooth. Rourke also knew they were lightweight, but for what he had in mind, he needed to sacrifice straightness for weight and energy transfer to his target. He needed some kind of weapon with standoff distance or reach, more than what the Sting provided if he was going to survive. Looking around, he found a stand of saplings next to the creek. He broke several off, twisting and pulling until they separated from their roots.

Each was a piece not quite a half-inch thick and about four feet long; then, he began hobbling along back on his escape path. Along the creek, he found a couple of rusted cans and two abandoned plastic milk bottles. Searching, he finally found a sheltered place he could work. With his black chrome Sting, he trimmed the twigs of the shafts and using the corner of a boulder smoothed the shafts until most of the knots disappeared.

Next, he cut a cross hatch groove in one end of each four inches down. He cut the plastic milk bottle into square pieces of about three and a half inches then sliced halfway through each. When he slid two pieces together at the slice, they formed a cross. This he slid into the cross hatch cuts he had made in the shafts to serve as flights or fletching.

Rourke removed his bootlaces, cut one in half, and re-laced both boots. Now, he would no longer have the ankle support of the severed laces, but they were long enough to at least close the shoe part of each boot and keep them on. He cut the tips off the other bootlace; a good bootlace is made similarly to paracord; there is a cover and inside several smaller strands of nylon.

He used some of the strands to secure the flights in each shaft. It took longer to flatten the rusted can and fatigue the metal, bending it back and forth until it gave; it was longer still before Rourke had four flattened pieces he could use as tips for the arrows. He shaped and sharpened these on a large rock before making cuts in the end of each arrow, inserted the points and secured them with the last of his small strands of nylon. He cut an angled notch in each arrow, a vertical cut toward the point and the notch angled up toward the flights.

Taking the bootlace cover, Rourke tied a knot in both ends. One knot was to keep the cover from unraveling, and the second was to launch the arrows; looking at his four weapons, he knew they were rough and weren't what you would call "pretty." As a kid however, Michael had been able to throw his "arrows" with accuracy into a round bale of hay at distances of 30 to 40 feet using man-sized silhouette targets, but that had been a long time ago. It was not much of a weapon, but it would have to do; now, he had to focus on the steps his father had taught him so long ago, the next steps of survival.

"STOP," his dad had said. "As soon as you realize you may be lost, stop, stay calm, and stay put until you have a plan. Usually, there is going to be nothing you can do about whatever got you to this point; focus now on solving problems of getting out of the situation." Michael knew that rescuers would be trying to find him but so would his attackers. The question was who would get to him first. It would probably be the bad guys.

"If you don't know where you are, taking off on foot means you have probably an 85 percent chance of being the wrong direction," John had said. "But, if you are not safe where you are, get to someplace safe, then stop. Sit down, take a drink of water, eat a handful of trail mix, and relax while you think things over." Michael wasn't just lost; he was under attack, and he had no trail mix. "Are you going north or south? Don't move at all until you have a definite reason to take a step."

Michael had no compass or a grid map, but he knew a little about the area he was in. He had three hours of daylight left. Rain was not on the forecast, but he needed water and shelter first; food would be nice but not essential right now.

His dad would have said, "Once you have determined the way to go and if you have time before dark, then go carefully." Michael knew a person could last about three minutes without air, three days without water, and three weeks without food. Dehydration was the most common physical condition in a survival situation, but he had found several creeks and runoffs; even if he cannot treat or filter the water, it was better to be sick a week from now rather than dead three days from now.

He had to marshal his strength and not work his body into a state of exhaustion. Right now, he realized he was experiencing adrenal letdown. The immediate threat had passed, and while the adrenaline had moved his body through the past several hours, he realized he was tired. He was going to have find or make a shelter where he could rest.

His father's words came back to him, "If you are tired, you're not effective, and you are more apt to become injured. Get as much rest as your body seems to need. When you are lost, the only resource you have is yourself."

Surveying his surroundings, he eliminated several potential shelter areas. He had pursuers trying to find him; his resting spot would have to be camouflaged. Spotting another possibility, Michael determined the safest path down a ravine. In the bottom of a ravine, he found another small stream and quenched his thirst. It took almost 45 minutes to navigate the steep terrain, but he found where he would camp.

A recent storm had caused the root system of a large tree to give way, falling; the trunk had landed on a large boulder and created a pocket underneath the canopy. He could not afford a fire, so he focused on collecting bedding and insulation. An hour later, he was finished and returned to the stream. Finding several discarded soft drink containers, he collected water and headed back to his shelter. His dad had said, "Sleeping is a survival task that rests your body and conserves energy."

Right now, the temperature was about 85 degrees, and it would drop close to 40 after the sun went down. Hypothermia was a threat if wet and he was. His body would get colder much faster, and he could die from hypothermia, even at 60 degrees. He emptied his bladder 20 feet away from the shelter and, before climbing in, positioned his water bottles where they would not spill.

Once inside, he removed his boots and socks, setting them to dry. He removed his flight suit and squeezed as much water as he could from the lower legs, drying his lower legs as best he could. Adjusting two branches he had prepared just for this purpose, he camouflaged the opening to his shelter and stretched out for a cat nap on a mattress of tree boughs, covering up with a blanket of leaves.

Thirty minutes passed before he slowly opened his eyes and listened. The sun had dropped low behind the hill he was on; the temperature was dropping. He redressed, thankful that most of the moisture had wicked away. His dad's words came back to him again, "Fear can motivate or paralyze; you need to control it, or it will control you. Every small thing makes survival a bit harder, and you don't need the extra challenge."

Redressed, rehydrated, hidden, and armed, Michael Rourke, President of the United States, spent the night listening, catnapping, and waiting to hear his enemies or his rescuers searching for him; when the sun crept across the ravine, the next day he was still waiting.

His dad would have said, "You've done good Son, but remember, every day you don't eat is another day you are consuming your body's stores and becoming weaker. Fortunately, you can go many days without food, but every day will see you weaker." Michael knew he had completed all the survival tasks he could early on, so he wouldn't be required to do them as he weakened.

Chapter Nineteen

"Okay," John Rourke said as he greeted the Secret Service team in front of his home. "Where is Tim Shaw?"

Frank Cole, the team leader, said, "He'll rendezvous with you at the first ambush site."

"The first?"

"Yes sir," Cole waved Rourke into the passenger seat. "I'm sending Agent Jack Bream with you." Rourke positioned his CAR-15 between his legs, muzzle down, and buckled up as Bream gassed the black SUV. "The convoy was hit twice; the President and trail vehicle made it out of the first one, but they were hit again a couple of miles further on."

"Casualties?"

"I don't have all of the details, Mr. Rourke," Bream admitted. "We have some agents who survived, several we know did not. We have two missing, your son and Agent Ken Farris. We have to assume they survived the attack."

Rourke nodded and picked up his cell phone, "Tim, your guy tried, he really did. But I'm coming and I want to be a part of finding my son."

Shaw said, "Let me talk to Bream." Rourke handed the phone to the agent.

"Sir, I'm sorry," Bream said.

"Forget it Jack, I've never been able to get John Rourke to mind either," Shaw said. "Just stick to him like glue. If he gets hurt, we both will suffer." Shaw wasn't concerned about the official problem, but he did not want to face his daughter Emma's wrath if Rourke was injured.

Bream closed the phone and said to Rourke, "Ken Farris is a good agent Mr. Rourke; he'll do his best to take care of your son."

"I know," was Rourke's final comment on the 30-minute drive.

*****

Shaw was waiting next to the broken guardrail; smoke still rose from the wreck and a second medical helicopter was landing. "John," Shaw said extending his hand as Rourke approached.

With Emma and the rest of the family safely under Secret Service protection, Rourke had commandeered an agent for backup and raced toward the scene of the ambush. Agent Jack Bream, following on Rourke's heels, feared his boss would probably give him a hard time for not being able to keep Rourke at home and under protection.

"What do we know, Tim?" Rourke asked, "How bad is it?"

"We had three who survived here; the driver died on impact. We've evacuated the two most seriously injured; one of them probably won't make it. Bill Manning is being debriefed," Shaw turned and pointed down the hill. "He's over there, minor injuries. The other vehicles followed protocol after the initial attack; they were hit again a few minutes further up there."

Looking in the direction Shaw had pointed, Rourke could see smoke rising from the second location. "Tim, get me over there," Rourke said jerking the charging handle on the CAR and setting the safety. Shaw motioned to Jack Bream, "Get him over to the second site and stick with him like ugly on an ape." Shaw keyed the microphone, "TACTICAL, this is Shaw, over."

"TACTICAL, go ahead, over." Anders came back.

"John Rourke is headed your way, leaving the scene as we speak. Just a head's up, over."

"Roger that. Any tips on how to handle him? Over," Anders asked.

"Straight up, Rourke doesn't have much tolerance for anything else, out," Shaw answered. Casting his gaze over the scene, Shaw dropped a Wrightism to the wind, "Wonder what happens if you get scared half to death twice?" and went to one of the AATVs.

Bream pulled over 100 yards back from the smoking debris; he pointed a man out and said, "That's Anders, Sir. You need to speak with him." Rourke nodded, exited the vehicle, and jogged over the SSAC.

"Agent Anders," Rourke said, extending his hand. "I'm John Rourke."

"Pleasure to meet you sir, but I wished it was under better conditions," Anders said returning the handshake.

"Lay it out for me," Rourke said.

"The second attack came from that direction," Anders said pointing to the south. "The first two energy blasts knocked both vehicles off the road and down the embankment. The third one destroyed the vehicles, creating the explosion and resulting fire. We have two missing, the President and Agent Ken Farris. There is no sign of either."

Rourke nodded, "Do we have eyes in the sky yet?"

"We do sir, but they haven't spotted anything yet. We don't know if the President and Farris were captured or are on the run. We do know they're unarmed; all of the agents' weapons have been accounted for, including Farris. Apparently in the violence of the crash, the weapons were knocked out of their hands, and I presume Farris just didn't have time to search for his. Fog of trauma or necessity because of the fire and need to get POTUS to safety, I can't really say. Maybe both I'd guess; Farris was a dedicated agent whose first responsibility was getting Michael Rourke to a safe position. That's what he did."

Rourke asked, "Can I get closer to the vehicles?"

Anders led the way down. Rourke made a cursory examination of both vehicles focusing on the ground before moving about 30 yards away and walking parallel to the scene on the north side. Cole turned to Anders, "What's he doing?"

"I'd say he's 'casting for sign,'" Anders said. "I believe he's trying to pick up their trail, he's tracking."

Rourke stopped and knelt down for a long minute before standing back up. "They went in that direction," he announced as he pulled the slung CAR-15 from his shoulder, double-checked the magazine and the safety, and started walking in that direction. Cole hurried to catch up with Rourke as Anders gave orders for two OSS teams to flank Rourke. Anders shook his head as he walked with one team, "We've been over this ground, and none of us saw a damn thing."

The team leader smiled and said simply, "None of us are John Thomas Rourke." About 45 minutes later, they recovered the body of Ken Farris. Rourke examined Farris and then turned to study the area. Finally, he leaned against a tree and lit a cigar; speaking softly, Rourke asked, "Where are you Son?"

Anders came over to Rourke, "Mr. Rourke?"

"Farris carried Michael most of the way," Rourke said. "He had to drag him the last few hundred yards but couldn't go on any further. Farris bled out internally, probably a partially ruptured spleen or damaged liver. He could have probably been saved if he had been able to get to a hospital. The autopsy will confirm that; I'm sure. Michael was probably knocked out during the attack and regained consciousness here when Farris stopped to rest."

Rourke studied the lay of the land trying to read Michael's plan. "Has there been any sign of the enemy at all?"

"No Sir, none," Anders said.

"Then, he'll evade and try to go to ground somewhere, particularly if he's injured," Rourke said. "He'll be headed in that direction."

"How can you be sure?" Anders asked.

"Because, that's what I would do."

Chapter Twenty

It was about 8:00 a.m. when President of the United States, Michael Rourke, awoke and listened. Peering through his cover, his eyes searched the area; the only sounds he heard belonged to nature. Satisfied that he was alone, he took a sip of water from the last rusty can; he was out again. Slowly and carefully he crawled out of the deadfall shelter until he could stand. His head hurt, and he was a little woozy; the blood seepage from his head wound had stopped again. Opening his flight suit, he pulled off his T-shirt.

"I should have done this yesterday," he said to himself cutting the bottom four inches of the shirt away with his knife before fashioning a headband out of it and bandaging the cut. He had swelling and trouble focusing his right eye. *"Probably a concussion,"* he thought as he wiggled back into the remainder of the shirt. Then, he stopped, listening.

Off in the distance, he thought he had heard the sound of a helicopter rotor, but he could not be sure; the sound had faded now. *"Well, the good guys are looking for me,"* he thought. He could feel the temperature increasing as the sun climbed higher in the sky. *"I figure I've got about a 75 percent chance of being located today,"* he thought before chuckling at something Tim Shaw had told him once, "42.7 percent of all statistics are made up on the spot."

Gathering his arrows after returning to the stream to fill up with water, Michael started east again. An hour later, the dark clouds had obscured the sun, and the rain started coming down with a vengeance. Another of Shaw's Wrightism came to mind as he stepped onto a dirt road cut through the hills, "If you want the rainbow, you gotta put up with the rain."

He was making better time on the road, but the road could be just as dangerous, if not more so. Taking the easiest way was not always the smartest plan; he knew he was exposed, but he also knew he had to help his rescuers, while trying to escape those who had attacked him. He was slightly nauseated and occasionally caught the taste of blood in his mouth. His back hurt on the left side; Michael unzipped his flight suit and shrugged the top down to reveal a healthy bruise that now reached from his shoulder blade to his waist. He slid his arms back into the flight suit and rezipped it; overall, he thought he was in pretty good shape.

Then, he saw it lying just off the road, a pineapple. He realized it must have bounced off a truck bringing a load to market. The pineapple is actually a multiple fruit, meaning each pineapple is actually made up of dozens of individual floweret's that grow together to form the entire fruit. He knew that pineapples stop ripening the minute they are picked; there is no special way of storing them that will help ripen them further. He also knew that smell is the most important thing in determining ripeness.

If a pineapple smells fresh, tropical and sweet, it will be a good fruit. The more "scales" a pineapple has, the sweeter and juicier the taste. Using his knife, he cut a chunk out and smelled it; it was fresh. He popped a piece in his mouth and began chewing. It was delicious. It was also medicinal. Bromelain, a proteolytic enzyme, is the key to a pineapple's value.

Bromelain is approved as a post-injury medication because it is thought to reduce inflammation and swelling. Orange juice is popular because it is high in vitamin C. Fresh pineapple is not only high in this vitamin, but the juice has an anthelmintic effect; it helps get rid of intestinal worms. The only downside is that the pineapple is also known to discourage blood clot development; between it and the sweat of his exertion, the cut on his head had begun leaking again by the time he had finished the fruit.

Thirty minutes passed, and Michael was off the dirt road, skirting it by about twenty yards when he heard the snap of a branch and the rustle of leaves. Michael stopped and listened, backed up against a large tree; slowly, he strung the arrow and waited. He knew he would only have one chance. Michael started "slicing the pie" to look around the tree; he could not afford to stick his head around all at once. That would present a target, and he had only one chance to pull this off. He wanted to keep a small profile by using the cover of the tree.

Expecting to see a black clad attacker, he instead saw a figure wearing civilian clothes and carrying a standard scoped hunting rifle, moving in a direction that would bring him within 10 yards of Michael's tree. *It must be a hunter*, Michael thought, breathing a sigh of relief. Then, the figure turned, and

Michael saw the face of Captain Timothy Dodd. He gripped the arrow tighter; he was being stalked.

Michael "sliced the pie" on the other side of the tree, spotting two others 20 and 40 yards away. They also were in civilian hunting clothes and carrying rifles with scopes. Armed only with his arrows, Michael could probably hit one; he might hit two, but assuring an instant kill with these primitive weapons was impossible. In any event, the third bad guy would almost certainly kill him. Michael also realized, as President of the United States, he could not surrender. Michael realized he was holding his breath and forced himself to breathe.

By now, Captain Dodd was 20 feet away and looking in another direction. Michael set his back foot and threw the arrow.

*****

John Thomas froze at the sound of the shot; it was a heavy caliber rifle report. He waved the teams forward as a second rifle fired, then a third.

The arrow hit Captain Dodd in the throat slicing through the left jugular and carotid arteries before stopping in the posterior section of the spinal column. It lodged between the second and third vertebrae after effectively slicing through the spinal cord. Dodd reflexively squeezed the trigger firing a round into the dirt at his feet then started collapsing; Michael was already in motion. He had to cover the distance before the other two could line up a shot; his target was no longer Dodd but Dodd's rifle.

Launching his own body, Michael knocked Dodd to the ground and grabbed the rifle, rolling downhill as fast as he could. The scope rifles were handicapping the shooters; the distance was too close for them to get a sight picture, and they were point firing. Michael rolled under another deadfall for cover and drew a bead on the closest attacker. The heavy rifle slug slammed low into the man's face, blowing a spray of bone and blood out behind him. The third attacker was advancing slowly and now was taking time to place his shots.

The heavy slugs were blowing chunks out of the rotten wood, and Michael was pinned down. His enemy continued to advance; Michael looked for a way out. There wasn't one. He tried firing blindly, but the attacker kept coming.

Finally, able to draw a bead on Michael's face the attacker said, "Mr. President, drop the weapon and please stand up. I will accept your surrender."

Michael dropped the rifle and slowly stood, his A.G. Russell Sting dagger gripped tightly in his right hand with the blade hidden alongside his forearm. He raised his left hand, "Right arm is broken I think." Michael walked around the left end of the deadfall. He had a plan, but it wasn't much of a plan; he would need to pull every trick out of his hat he could. If he could not close fast enough, he could make his enemy kill him, and that was preferable to surrender. Surrender was something Michael Rourke could have contemplated, not the President of the United States. Standing there dirty, injured, unarmed, and looking totally defeated, he did not present an imposing, threatening, or intimidating figure. His captor held the rifle in his right hand and supported himself with his left as he took a step on the uneven terrain.

Michael continued to move to his opponent's right side; his dad had grilled it into him, "If a shooter is right-handed and you are facing him, move to your left; if he or she is left-handed, move to your right. It's harder to swing your arm and body away from the direction of the firing hand and shoot accurately."

As soon as he saw the rifle move off-target and his enemy take a step, Michael moved, the Sting flashing upward in a reverse grip aiming for the left side of the man's neck. He heard a shot ring out, and he knew he had failed.

Chapter Twenty-One

John Rourke had dropped to his knees and crawled the last six feet to the top of the hill and peered over. He spotted the attacker advancing toward Michael; he flipped the CAR-15 safety lever to fire and drew a bead on the man's chest. Michael slowly stood and raised his left arm; his right hung limply at his side as he walked slowly around the log he had used for cover. John sized up the situation in a glance, and he saw Michael's plan.

As Michael's captor advanced, he steadied himself with his left hand on a tree that's when Michael made his move. John shouted, "Akiro Kuriname!" and fired. The attacker glanced up toward Rourke then tried to track his weapon on Michael; he fired and missed. The attacker looked back toward Michael just as the desperate leap slammed Michael's body into him. John's round missed, but Michael's charge knocked the attacker over backwards; a heavy thud sounded when the man's head impact a large rock.

John Rourke charged down the hill toward his son, slinging the CAR-15 and drawing his fighting Bowie from the sheath at the middle of his back. "You okay?" John asked, and Michael nodded. John Rourke looked at the attacker who had not moved. Blood had splattered when his head impacted on the rock and obscured his face as he lay still and unconscious. John ripped open the attackers shirt and with the point of the Bowie started cutting.

Michael stared in shock and shouted, "Dad, what are you doing?"

"The same procedure for what is called an excisional biopsy. I'm taking his tattoo off. Remember what happened to the Captain Dodd clone we captured? His autopsy showed there was a chemical contained in his tattoo that killed him. We still don't know how it was activated. I believe this tattoo forms some kind of link between the individual clones and the alien force. If he regains consciousness, the aliens can use him as a transmitter to monitor what is occurring. When they wish, they simply activate the chemical and kill him."

With the outline of the tattoo sliced into the skin, Rourke pulled a Leatherman multi-tool from his pocket and, grabbing an edge of skin, started slicing the connective tissue under the tattoo with the razor edge of the Bowie, while Michael collected the discarded rifle.

"Whatever you hollered at him worked," Michael said. "I thought he had me, but his shot went wild; when he looked up, he didn't have time for a second shot."

Supervisory Special Agent John Anders rushed up to them, knelt, and grabbed Michael's shoulder, "You okay, Mr. President?"

"Yes," Michael said. Anders grabbed his microphone and started issuing orders. He called for a medic to examine Michael and sent the rest of his team to set up an overwatch securing the area. He started directing the rest of the force to scour the area for any additional enemy forces.

"Dr. Rourke, what are you doing?" Anders asked disgustedly.

"Give me a minute and I will explain," Rourke said. "We need this guy to give us answers." When he was finished, Rourke sat back and said to the medic who had finished his examination of Michael and had dropped down on one knee by Rourke's side, "I've removed a large area of skin. I did a procedure called an excisional biopsy, same way we take a sample for a cancer biopsy of a large area of skin. I need you to cover the excised area with a bandage and check the head wound. He's unconscious, and I want to keep him that way for a while. I need you to tell me if he's going to survive."

Rourke turned to Anders and asked, "Do you have a plastic bag?" Anders opened a pouch and pulled a plastic evidence bag. Then, he handed it to Rourke. John placed the sample inside and sealed it. "Okay, Anders I need this man and this sample secured. When he fell, he hit his head on that rock which knocked him out. He's going to need medical treatment for that and for this," Rourke said pointing at his handiwork. "I want him transported to a secure medical facility as soon as possible, and I want him under guard 24/7."

Anders nodded and spoke into his microphone again.

"Dad, what was it you shouted?"

John Rourke wiped the blade of the Bowie on the man's shirt, removing the blood before securing it in the sheath. "I said, 'Akiro Kuriname.'"

"What does it mean?" Michael asked.

"It's his name Michael," Rourke said. "Akiro Kuriname was part of the Eden Project crew for Eden 3, remember?"

"Yeah, I remember," Michael answered after a short pause. "His Captain was Jane Harwood, and the Medical Officer was Elaine Halverson. So, we definitely have another clone?"

"Yes, we do," said his father. "That's a damn shame. Akiro, the original, was a good man and a good friend. I wished they hadn't done this to him."

The medic examined the head wound first, put a cervical collar on the unconscious man, then turned to the bloody wound on his left upper chest. First, flushing the area with an antiseptic wash, he applied a bandage to cover the wound. "Mr. Rourke?" the medic said as he turned. Both Michael and John answered, "Yes." John smiled at the medic, "Sorry, we do that a lot. What's your verdict?"

"He has a depressed skull fracture," the medic said. "That's not a good thing; we need to get an x-ray and get him to surgery as soon as possible. The brain will already be swelling, and we have to remove the pressure as soon as possible. That's what I can tell you right now, Mr. Rourke; I can't say he'll survive. The neurosurgeon will have to make that call, but I believe the head trauma is the only injury. Or, I should say was the only injury until you started cutting on him."

Anders keyed his microphone. The medic dug in his pack, pulling out and unfolding a field litter with handles heavily stitched along each side of the foldable stretcher. Carefully, with John's help, he stabilized the unconscious man's neck, and then, they rolled him onto the stretcher. Anders sat on the ground with an area map stretched out before him. He gave the chopper pilot the coordinates and selected two of his strongest men to transport Akiro Kuriname to the landing zone.

John and Michael joined the carry crew grabbing the handles toward the unconscious man's feet, and two escorts accompanied the team to provide security. Anders primary missions were to secure the President and to attempt contact with any enemy forces still in the area; he had accomplished the first and now set out to coordinate a further attempt at the second.

*****

By the time the chopper had arrived at the King Kamehameha Trauma Center, Natalia and a squad of Secret Service agents had commandeered an entire floor of Honolulu's main hospital. Dressed in a black body suit and high-topped leather boots, she ran to Michael as soon as he cleared the chopper's rotor arch and as soon as his unconscious attacker had been placed on a gurney; they were escorted to a private room on the commandeered fifth floor. Michael was checked over by the presidential physician and declared fit, except for a little dehydration and minor exposure, before they moved upstairs. He would be spending at least one night.

His attacker was rushed to the third floor neurosurgery department where he was x-rayed and taken directly to the surgical suite. Tim Shaw arrived and joined John Rourke outside the neurosurgery suite where an operation was already in progress to relieve the pressure from Akiro Kuriname's swollen brain and repair the damage to his skull. "Our teams have searched the area around the two hits," Shaw said. "Nothing was found except the vehicle that brought that hunter team into the area after Michael."

Rourke nodded, "That doesn't surprise me. What does surprise me is they were not so much interested in killing Michael as capturing him. I still haven't figured out what their game is."

Chapter Twenty-Two

Phillip Greene, the former Progressive presidential candidate, and his "fellow travelers" sat in the War Room of the party headquarters. The War Room was routinely swept for bugs and electronic surveillance; no one could be privileged to the conversations of this group. Every person, excepting Greene, had insinuated themselves into sensitive positions within the government. They were the ones who fed Greene information. At the far end of the large conference table sat Greene's primary advisor, the man known as Captain Dodd.

Greene, red-faced with the veins pulsing in his forehead, slammed his fist into the table, "What the hell went wrong? The plan was perfect. A low-level trip for a public relations visit, a wide open area, and we still missed. What the hell went wrong?" His "team" squirmed in their chairs.

Finally, a man in uniform spoke; Brigadier General Jimmy "JJ" Jones said, "Sir, it should have worked. The plan was tight. If we had brought my forces in instead of Captain Dodd's men, we would have been successful; no offense Captain Dodd. We simply could have put more boots on the ground."

Dodd smiled, "None taken, General. You may be right; we simply won't know now. Had we been successful that would have moved our agenda forward; it ended up being more of a non-event, didn't it? The good news is we learned something without giving our enemies an upper hand. Our attack craft was not detected, and our ground forces were eliminated without giving up any information."

"You're sure?" Greene asked with sweat rolling down his pudgy cheeks.

"Yes, I'm sure," Dodd said. "My Principal has assured me that all contact was lost with the hunter team. That only occurs when the 'units' are terminated. Unfortunately, we gained nothing of intelligence value; fortunately, neither did the governmental forces. I believe that concludes our meeting for today." Dodd stood and exited the room, leaving everyone somewhat stunned with their dismissals.

Phillip Greene caught the eye of General Jones and, with a nod of his head, indicated he needed to speak with The General. When the others had left, Jones came over and sat by Greene, "Yes Sir, you wanted to speak with me?"

Greene nodded, "JJ, I don't like how this is playing out. I don't think we have enough control. Damn it, we should have made a clean sweep on this operation. Instead, Michael Rourke is still functioning, and we look like idiots."

Jones shook his head, "Not us, we cannot be tied to this operation. Somebody looks like an idiot, but no one can point a finger at us."

"True," Greene said wiping his mouth with a now ever-present white handkerchief. "But, the reality is the operation was a failure; we're in the same boat we were three days ago. That is just damned unacceptable." He still had difficulty preventing drool from dripping from the left side of the jaw Michael had dislocated. Doctors told him there had been nerve damage that might take months to heal, if it ever did.

Chapter Twenty-Three

Rourke sat in the waiting room examining his hands; he had washed his hands in the restroom upon arrival, but as he sat, he kept noticing residual blood in the nail beds and creases of his skin. He scrounged some alcohol swabs from the nurse and was spending the time removing the blood from his hands and the Bowie blade. The delicate operation had gone on for almost four hours when the lead neurosurgeon came out to the waiting room and asked for Dr. Rourke.

"I'm John Rourke; what's the verdict doctor?"

"Dr. Rourke, I'm Dr. Johnson," he said removing his surgery cap. It and the front of his scrubs were soaked with his own perspiration. "As you know, the primary goals for brain injury treatment are to stop any bleeding, prevent an increase in pressure within the skull, control the amount of pressure should an increase occur, maintain adequate blood flow to the brain, and remove any large blood clots or fragments of the skull. I had to perform a hemicraniectomy, temporarily removing a portion of the skull in order to allow the swollen brain to expand beyond the confines of the skull bone, without causing further elevations in brain pressure. We will keep that part of the skull bone frozen until the swelling has resolved, at which point it can be sutured back onto its original place."

"We have accomplished those tasks. Now, we will keep the head of the bed elevated slightly and the neck brace on to keep it straight. This should help decrease the intracranial pressure by allowing blood and cerebrospinal fluid to drain from the brain."

"I've ordered the limit on the fluids a patient receives. As you know, the brain is like a sponge; it swells with extra fluid. Limiting fluids will help control the swelling. We will keep him on diuretics to decrease the amount of water in the patient's body which will make less water available to the brain to cause swelling. I also have him on anticonvulsants to prevent seizures that can result from extra electrical activity in the brain. We're actually picking up some brain activity which frankly I cannot explain."

"Any idea when he'll regain consciousness, Doctor?" Rourke asked.

"I can't guarantee that he will; further, I cannot guarantee what shape his mind will be in; I believe we may have damage to two areas. The initial injury occurred to the parietal lobe which controls tactile sensation, response to internal stimuli, sensory comprehension, some language, reading, and some visual functions. Additionally, due to the direction of impact, a sliver of the skull bone was driven into the frontal lobe which controls attention, behavior, abstract thinking, problem solving, creative thought, emotion, intellect, initiative, judgment, coordinated movements, muscle movements, smell, physical reactions, and personality. I can't say if damage has been done or how much until, and if, he wakes up."

Tim Shaw approached from behind Rourke and asked, "What do you think his chances are?"

"I can't even hazard a guess," the Doctor said. "I've done all I can do for the head injury. I'm still concerned about the wound to his chest and the possibility of infection from that. Who removed that five-inch by five-inch piece of skin?"

"I did Doc," Rourke admitted. "I can't explain, but it was necessary."

"What the hell did you use," the surgeon asked incuriously, "a butcher knife?"

Rourke cast his eyes toward the floor and shook his head, "Nope, a Bowie. It was the only thing I had. Did you receive the sample of his skin I removed?"

Shaw interrupted, "No John, that sample was received by my people and has been taken for analysis per your instructions. It's considered evidence right now, and our lab people are trying to determine if it works the way you suspect it does. Do you really think it forms some type of a kill switch that can be controlled remotely?"

"I do Tim. I can't be sure, but I think so. I just don't know how it works. I believe that is what happened to the last Captain Dodd we ran into. It just makes sense that, somehow, someone wanted him dead and was able to activate something with his tattoo that made that happen. I hope we can find out what that something is."

Chapter Twenty-Four

The Keeper arrived at John Rourke's house that evening. "John, I came as soon as I heard. How is your son?"

"He's fine, Sir. Thanks for coming." Rourke wasn't quite sure what it was, but the more he was around and listened to The Keeper, the more intrigued he became. The Keeper seemed almost to exude peace and harmony, yet this was tempered by an internal strength. Rourke wanted to know more about The Keeper's experience and understanding of "Life," a life that had continued uninterrupted longer than anyone other than the rest of the KI.

By conventional standards, the KI lifespan was already significantly longer than humans. Adding to that, the time spent traveling at almost the speed of light had extended that life over 40,000 human years; The Keeper, however, only appeared to be in his late seventies or early eighties. Still vibrant, purposeful, and intelligent, The Keeper offered Rourke a most unique opportunity for a "lay-cultural anthropological study."

Rourke and The Keeper adjourned to the patio outside. The Keeper gathered his robe garment and sat. "John, I realize that now is probably not the best time to have this conversation, but I believe there are some things you need to hear."

Rourke nodded and sat. "Keeper, surely in your long experience you have come to some deeper understandings about 'Life,' about being 'Human?'"

The Keeper smiled and looked at Rourke with both a deep compassion and understanding; it was a warm and accepting look. Rourke felt the presence of The Keeper again; it seemed to give Rourke a feeling of comfort and clarity of purpose.

"From the perspective of being Human," The Keeper began, "here is my simplest understanding. You, John Thomas Rourke, are a self-aware consciousness incarnate in a physical reality. You, more so than most men, have created and co-created your personal reality. You are part of what you call 'Life' and that 'Life' is constantly changing, constantly evolving, and constantly becoming more."

Rourke let The Keeper's words sink in for a while as he sat quietly. Leaning back, he pulled a small cigar from his shirt pocket and, with his Zippo, lit it. The Keeper said, "May I try one of those?" Rourke smiled and, when both of the cigars were lit, said, "Be careful; if you inhale, you may find yourself a little light-headed. What do you mean by, 'I have created and co-created my personal reality?'"

The Keeper seemed to be focused simply on puffing the cigar but said, "By your beliefs, your fears, and your unresolved issues, you are much like a magnet and pull experiences to yourself to either fulfill yourself or to put you in a position to deal with these issues, hopefully growing and learning from them. Life itself is 'creativity expressed' and this creativity exists in each self-aware consciousness. There is a natural desire for evolution in consciousness that will continue to bring any unresolved issues into your awareness until you effectively deal with them in a way that contributes to your growth. This can be called, 'Movement.'"

"The more fears and unresolved issues you deal with and put behind you, the more room there is for experiences that will bring you further joy and fulfillment. There are no secrets to this, there is no defined process, and there is no secret handshake to facilitate it. Each piece of consciousness comes to their own truth in their own time. As with 'Life' itself, that 'Movement' simply just 'IS.'"

After a short pause he continued, "Now, with respect to co-creating reality, just as each person creates that portion of their own reality, the gestalt of group consciousness does the same thing. It co-creates the reality that the larger population experiences, from local aspects right up to worldly 'learnings' or 'knowings.'"

Rourke thought to himself, *Yeah right, we create our own reality! And, what about all the things that others are doing to us and all the mean, inconsiderate, or terrible things that happen; the stuff that is out of our control, out of our ability to prevent.* He framed the thought into a question. "It seems that there are others out there doing things to us that we have not asked for or that we don't deserve. What about these experiences?"

The Keeper nodded and inhaled the cigar smoke tentatively; slowly exhaling, the smoke drifted up on a breeze. "I find this ritual rather relaxing, as do I find your company. Remember, each individual or group of consciousness has either drawn an experience to itself through its beliefs or by the desire to experience the occurrence with the 'knowing' that it will offer an increase of their understanding and, as a result, an increase in the quality of their consciousness. Quite often, this understanding is at a soul level and may not exist within the conscious knowledge of the entities involved."

Rourke responded, "Well, let's just simplify things. Ponder on this; at the moment, I'm dealing with some race of aliens cloning Commander Dodd to take control of the earth. We have KI who want to control the Earth and feel they have the right to do so because they used to live here, we have earth citizens who have been here for the last 50,000 years evolving to their current state and feel it is their world to control, and we have people, such as you, who seem to accept each and all in equal ways. How does this fit into each soul drawing these experiences to itself?"

The Keeper smiled and said, "All consciousness has the same potential; there will be either consequences or benefits, most likely both. But, not all consciousness is at the same level of understanding. Imagine yourself describing some specialized heart surgery procedure to a youth in junior high school. They could hear your words and would know what a heart was but would have no practical way to bring more of an understanding at the moment. It does not mean they are any less, just that they are not yet perceiving things in that way. Yet, they may become a doctor in later years and then understand it perfectly. Perception is relative."

He went on, "The same holds true for consciousness as a whole. Much of that which is incarnate is still in a sort of survival stage, and to them, all other consciousness is 'other' and is to be feared. Some of the 'others' are good, and some are bad, both again being very subjective and in relative terms. This includes most of the aliens involved openly with your civilization at this time."

"Then, there are the more aggressive of the KI. Although they know we are all related, they concentrate on the differences. Using their own feeling of entitlement, they would dominate earth citizens if given the chance. Other KI have come to the awareness that we are all interrelated and would work towards the good of all involved."

"Then, you have entities such as me; in my own time, we were many, but that was before we left this world. Today, there are many on Earth such as I; I can feel them, sense them if you will. We understand the Oneness of all consciousness and that we only draw to us those experiences that help us to grow. As a result, we are closed to none and welcome the ongoing process of Life. It is called unity-consciousness."

The Keeper paused and then said, "But, that is enough for now. I would recommend you sleep on it and only incorporate those things that intuitively ring true to you. Only take in that which feels right to you at an intuitive level. So, what constitutes these levels of consciousness, and how do they manifest in the human form?"

The Keeper continued, "These perspectives of consciousness relate to energy flows in the physical body. A physical manifest or incarnated entity has seven energy centers. The top, or highest, and the bottom, or lowest, are fixed and constitute being incarnate in physical reality. The upper ties into the soul level. The lower binds us to the physical or, in most normal earthlings, the Earth."

"As consciousness is light, the centers relate to the refracted colors of white light, as in a rainbow. The color associated with the highest center is violet and the lowest, or base, is red. In between are increasing vibration centers that relate to orange, yellow, green, blue, and indigo. The energy balance and intensity between these centers and the amount of energy that flows through each is indicative of the level of consciousness and balance achieved by the individual person; the higher the vibration of light, the higher the level or quality of consciousness."

The Keeper went on, "The alien entities that are cloning Dodd are functioning very much in what is called a 'service to self' focus and could care less about the other consciousness they encounter. They act on what is to their advantage and their best interest. Some of the KI have moved beyond this and have chosen a path we call 'service to others.' They no longer wish to control others but have yet to see how we are all interrelated. To them, there is still 'us and them.'"

"A few others here on earth, and some not of earth, have moved onto a unity style of consciousness and realize there is only one Source that is fragmented into countless, separate individual pieces of consciousness. They realize that all is interrelated and every piece of consciousness is experiencing the perfect experience needed for their growth at that moment in the evolution of 'All That Is.'" The Keeper paused for a moment, as if to let what he had just spoken sink into Rourke's mind.

Rourke, who had been listening with his head down, looked up and asked, "How many earthlings are working at this level of unity-consciousness?"

"I have used your computers recently, and my research has shown me this movement towards unity-consciousness started over again in your world during the latter portions of the last millennium and has gained momentum ever since. Those were the troubling times experienced by many between 1950 and what you call the Night of the War. They reflected the letting go of old paradigms that no longer served a useful purpose."

"Financial institutions, political systems, and governments experienced the greatest change; as they had been very focused on 'service to self'; seemingly without care for the rest of humanity. In the early decades of the new millennium, earthly consciousness finally passed the point of balance where the overall consciousness of earth was slightly more positive than negative."

The Keeper went on, "Right now, there are various probabilities coming into play that will offer varied futures for many. Those who have held steadfast in their 'service to self' or controlling realities will continue to experience this. Those who have used their experiences and 'learnings' to come to a better understanding of unity-consciousness will move into that experience. There is a certain momentum or movement that occurs. In physics, it is called a quantum leap."

Rourke said, "You mention light quite often in reference to consciousness. What is the importance of light, or better yet, what role does light play in consciousness?"

The Keeper smiled and replied, "From a larger, more encompassing perspective, light is all there is. I am not speaking of just the visible spectrum but the entire spectrum of energy, which is also in fact light. Consciousness is that light fragmented into individual, self-aware units of which I am one and you are one. The perception or individual experience of this light is greatly slowed down in the physical plane, and it is this that gives us the ability to perceive this reality as solid."

"To give you an idea of what I mean by slowed down, look at the Atomic Clock used to document official time. It uses the oscillation frequency of the cesium atom which is 9,192,631,770 Hertz, or cycles per second. That is over nine billion vibrations per second. Now, this is just one of the measurements we use in physical reality; you can imagine the speed that exists in the reality from which this physical reality springs."

"All physical phenomena in this reality can be traced back in this same way. The speed of light has a distinct reason for being the speed it is and why it is always consistent to observers in a common space-time position. But, these are talks for another time," said The Keeper, "and I have a meeting with the President of New Germany. Good evening, and may your dreams be comforting. We'll speak more tomorrow." With that, he got up and stopped, grasping the back of the bench unsteadily, "I see what you mean about inhaling and the light-headedness." Regaining his balance, he turned and left. Rourke finished the cigar and for a long time just sat there, thinking about The Keeper's words and listening to the crashing of the waves.

Chapter Twenty-Five

His first awakening was barely a memory now. His regaining of consciousness was not a struggle; one moment he "was not," and the next moment he "was." His mind had been buffeted with many impressions all at once. Light, fear, heat, and pain cascaded over him like a waterfall; then, he "was not" again.

He did not know how long he "was not;" his next awareness hit him with the realization he could not move nor was he where he should have been even though his mind could not articulate where that was supposed to be.

When his third awareness manifested itself, he simply laid still, keeping his eyes closed and his breathing rhythmic. In his mind's eye, he assessed his bodily conditions. His head hurt, he could not move, something had been forced down his throat, and his limbs had been tied down; in the distance, he could hear an insistent beeping that was growing faster. Slowly, he opened his eyes; he thought he must be in sickbay, but he had no idea of how he had gotten there.

He recognized the obstruction in his throat; he had been intubated; a breathing tube had been put into his windpipe through his nose and now resided in his throat. He still had no idea why he had needed the endotracheal tube. A nurse came to his beside, "You're awake. That is very good. I will alert the Doctor." *Good,* he thought. His medical officer, Elaine Halverson, will explain all of this to him. Then, he slipped back into nothingness.

Dr. Johnson was examining the patient when he regained consciousness the next time. "Good morning; I am pleased you are with us again. My name is Dr. Johnson. You have been a challenging patient. Can you tell me your name?"

Akiro Kuriname swallowed realizing his throat was sore and also that the endotracheal tube had been removed. He had to swallow a couple of more times before he could speak, "Water." His voice was scratchy. Dr. Johnson reached for a glass of water and positioned it so the bent straw was within the reach of his lips.

"Just a sip for right now, you can have more in a few moments."

"My name is Lieutenant Akiro Kuriname; I am a crew member of Eden 3. What happened? Where is Dr. Halverson? She is the medical officer on my crew," the man squeaked.

"I'm not at liberty to discuss that with you Mr. Kuriname, but I've sent for someone who can. Right now, I need you to rest." Kuriname watched as the doctor injected a syringe into an IV line, and sleep came to him once more.

When Kuriname awoke again, he saw a man standing over by the window looking out; he was vaguely familiar. John Thomas Rourke felt Kuriname's eyes on him and turned to face the bed. "Good afternoon, Akiro."

"I'm sorry; you look familiar, but do I know you?"

"In a manner of speaking, you and I met a long time ago, but the circumstances were rather unusual," Rourke said pulling a chair near the bed. "My name is John Thomas Rourke, and we have a lot to go over. The story probably is not going to make a lot of sense to you. We can continue to talk more later if you find you are tiring. What is important for you to know is that you are safe and you're with friends who are going to take care of you."

Dr. Johnson was checking the bandaged wound on his chest. "How did I get that wound, doctor?" Akiro asked. "Was it the accident?"

"No Sir," Johnson said. "There was no accident, but it appears this probably saved your life, and you have John Rourke to thank for that. He removed a rather large section of skin from your chest; that is all I can say about that right now. Dr. Rourke may explain it in more detail. Your skin is actually made up of several layers. The epidermis, or outermost layer, is what we see, and it provides a protective, waterproof seal over the body. Below that is the dermis which contains sweat glands, hair follicles, blood vessels, and more. The hypodermis or subcutaneous layer lies below the skin and is made up of loose connective and adipose or fat tissues."

"The hypodermis binds the skin to underlying organs, while allowing the skin to move somewhat independently of underlying structures. Adipose tissue in the hypodermis provides padding and shock absorption that helps to protect underlying tissues from damage; it is also important in insulating against loss of body heat. This is where the slicing occurred; Dr. Rourke was able to remove the affected area without any permanent damage. The synthetic skin graft is already mending the wound and regenerating the adipose tissue he removed."

Rourke asked, "Akiro, how are you feeling?"

"Confused, tired, and strangely..." Akiro Kuriname searched for the right word. "Strangely alone."

"That, my friend, is better news than I could have expected," Rourke said. As Kuriname watched, Dr. Johnson pressed the plunger on another syringe, and his eyes grew heavy. The last thing he heard was Rourke saying, "We'll talk more in the morning, and I'll explain it all to you."

*****

The next morning, Rourke stuck his head in the door, "Good, you're awake. Good morning, Dr. Johnson; how's our patient doing today?"

"Morning Dr. Rourke, he is doing very well. I'll leave you two alone; I believe he has some questions for you," Dr. Johnson said.

Kuriname waved Rourke in and said, "I definitely do."

"Akiro," Rourke asked, "what is the last thing you remember before waking up here?"

Kuriname closed his eyes and thought, then said, "The last clear memory I have is after we left Earth orbit to start the Eden mission and I was lying down in the cryogenic chamber; that's the last clear one. However, there are bits and pieces that I think are memories, but they don't make any sense; they could just be dreams I had in the sleep."

Rourke nodded, "What kind of dreams?"

Kuriname thought, closing his eyes, the effort to drag something out of the depths of his memories or his dreams showed as his brow furrowed, "Another room, similar to this one but very different. I think it was something medical, but I can't be sure. There is the feeling of being connected to something or someone."

"But, you don't feel that connection now?" Rourke asked.

"No, I can't even define what the connection was or even how to describe how it felt, but it is gone."

"Akrio," Rourke said, "the Eden Project returned to Earth, a long time ago. It's been over 600 years since you launched."

Kuriname shook his head, "How is that possible, and why don't I remember the landing? Did this head wound zap my memory? Do I have amnesia?"

"No, Akiro, it is a lot more complicated than that," Rourke said as he reached over and placed a comforting hand on Kuriname's shoulder.

"Akiro, I've done a lot of thinking about how to 'catch you up' on the current situation, but there's no easy or gentle way to do that. You deserve the truth, but I warn you that it is not an easy or pleasant truth. Based on what I think I know about you, I believe you can handle it though," Rourke said standing to face the window leaving Kuriname with his own thoughts.

Several minutes passed before Akiro Kuriname finally said, "Okay, tell me the truth. Give it all to me now and don't hold anything back. Once I know what the reality is, I'll deal with it."

Rourke spoke softly, "First of all, the Eden Project was a success. The shuttle fleet completed their mission and returned 500 years after the Night of the War, but the world was still in turmoil; in fact, one Eden crew member died within the first 24 hours of their return. The evils that had plunged our world into darkness still existed, and the fight went on for some time after Eden's return. The crews of the original Eden project have all been dead now for over 100 years," Rourke looked at Kuriname.

"A friend of my daughter, a PhD candidate at the University of Mid-Wake named Amanda Welch, recently made an amazing discovery. Her thesis on theoretical astrophysics had allowed her, as part of the work, to be able to examine the electronic logs of the original Eden Project's 500-year voyage. Amanda found an anomaly; the Eden Project flight had been interrupted, and the entire fleet of ships remained in a geosynchronous orbit around something. She still has no idea what, but the fleet remained stationary for nearly three terrestrial years before it was allowed to continue on. No one understood the significance of that find until recently."

"A few months ago, my wife Emma and I were attacked while we were on an archaeological dive in the Mediterranean. One of the attackers was positively identified as Captain Timothy Dodd, Commander of Eden 1."

"But, you said the original crews had died over 100 years ago," Kuriname was shaken.

"That is correct; the original crews died," Rourke paused for a moment to let that sink in. Rourke stepped to the bed and clasped hands with Kuriname, "The attacker was Captain Dodd's clone. You asked if we knew each other; I met Akiro Kuriname when Eden landed. We became good friends and fought together several times; I called him my friend."

Three seconds went by, then ten, and then twenty as Kuriname processed the information. Suddenly, Kuriname's grip increased so strong it was painful to Rourke; he feared his own hand would be broken.

"You're telling me...," Kuriname said slowly between clenched teeth. "You're telling me that I'm not real, that I'm not Akiro Kuriname, and that I'm some kind of freak, a clone?"

"No, I'm telling you that you ARE Akiro Kuriname, with all of his DNA, all of his memories, and most importantly, all of his strength and honor. Eden 3 crewman, Japanese naval test pilot, Lt Akiro Kuriname was my friend, and I grieved at his loss. I want you to become my friend; I need your help. I want to celebrate your rebirth."

Tears began to roll down Kuriname's face; he released Rourke's hand, "How did I get here? What is going on? Who am I?"

Stepping back from the bed and rubbing his hand to restore the feeling in it, Rourke faced Kuriname and said, "Here is what I believe. During that sleep, genetic material was removed from all of the crew members of the Eden Project. I have already encountered two Captain Dodds; I suspect there are many more. The tissue I removed from your chest was in the form of a tattoo."

"I believe that tattoo, and we don't understand how, enabled the entities that created the duplicates to control them, bend their wills to the entities own nefarious agendas, and if they are captured, to terminate the duplicates. I gambled on the fact that if that tattoo was removed the bond and control would be terminated and your own personality, morality, and ethics would be returned. It appears I was correct. That means if it worked on you it could conceivably work on the others."

"The Eden Project personnel were picked because they were the best candidates to save the human race. The original Captain Dodd must have had personality traits that circumstances perverted, and his psychopathic side emerged." Rourke paused. "I'm one of the very few who had the opportunity to deal with both the original Dodd and the original Akiro Kuriname. Dodd was flawed; you weren't. Dodd tried to destroy mankind; Akiro died to save it. I know this is a lot to absorb. I don't know if I could make sense out of it."

"My goal was to rescue you from enslavement as a clone. I will tell you this; I was duplicated, and my duplicates were to be used against humanity," Rourke said. "I did not allow that; don't allow yourself to be used against your own people. You have a second chance, Akiro; use that second chance. Be who you are. Be Akiro Kuriname, and help us save your brothers and sisters from Eden. Lieutenant Kuriname, finish this mission; no one else can."

Chapter Twenty-Six

"Good Morning, Akiro," John Rourke said after opening the hospital room door. "How are you feeling?"

Kuriname looked up from the magazine and did not answer but waved Rourke inside the room. Folding the magazine closed, he laid it on the bed stand and sat up a little bit. "I'm okay. In fact, they are going to release me today; I suspect that means I'm headed for a jail cell somewhere."

"Nope, I don't think so," Rourke said turning and reaching outside to retrieve two packages. "Here, this is for you," Rourke said setting the small package on the bed next to Kuriname. "I think they'll fit. The clothes you were wearing are still being held for evidence."

It contained running shoes, underwear, socks, and an athletic suit that was yellow with black trim. "Ah, very nice, this is just like what Bruce Lee wore. I like it. What's that?"

Rourke held up the other package; it was longer and narrower, "This, it's a surprise for later. Let's get you outta here. The doctors have signed your release, and you are officially in my 'custody.' Change clothes and let's go."

Ten minutes later, the nurse had rolled Kuriname down in the mandatory wheelchair. He stood and walked slowly to Rourke's vehicle. "Where are we going?"

"You'll see," Rourke said. Twenty minutes later, they pulled up to Rourke's beachfront home. "Here's where you'll be staying for a while, my house."

"It sure looks better than the jail cell I had envisioned," Kuriname said and followed Rourke to the front door. Emma opened it and said, "Mr. Kuriname, welcome to our home."

Akiro bowed and said, "Thank you for your graciousness Mrs. Rourke." Not sure how to proceed, he stumbled and started to ask, "Have we..."

"No," Rourke said. "Emma was not in my life at that time." Filling in the blank that Emma had not met the original Akiro Kuriname, Kuriname nodded.

"Emma will show you to your room; then, meet me on the patio. Honey, could you bring us some drinks out there? I have to set something up."

Ten minutes later, Emma opened the door as Akiro carried the tray with drinks. "John," he said, "I love your home, and your wife is most gracious. Thank you again."

"Akiro, come here please," Rourke gestured to a cleared area next to the table. Kuriname complied, and Emma set the tray on the table. "Akiro Kuriname, I have something that belongs to you, and I believe now is the time to return it." Emma stood to one side, and Rourke reached under the table and removed the long box. Slicing through the tape at one end, he directed Kuriname to face away and look at the house. Kuriname again complied but this time with a confused look on his face.

Rourke withdrew the bag, untied the cord sliding the object out of the bag, and positioned himself behind Kuriname. "Akiro Kuriname, I return this to you."

When Akiro turned around, he saw Rourke kneel on one knee with his arms extended forward and his head bowed. Akiro was stunned, "It.... it cannot be." He said with his voice choking. "It is...," he said. "It is Saiai no hōmotsu. It is my Beloved Treasure." Akiro took the sword from Rourke and with his right hand drew it partially from its sheath. "How John, how did you do this?"

Rising to his feet, Rourke said, "When my friend Akiro died so long ago, I recovered this and have kept it in my family since. I never thought I would get this opportunity; now it is returned to its rightful owner. I never had the ideogram engraving translated. Now I know what it means, don't I?"

"Yes, she is called Beloved Treasure," Akiro said as tears rolled down his face. "Never did I expect to see her again. John Rourke, thank you. I pledge my eternal friendship to you and your family. I pledge also to stand with you in any battle at any time."

最愛の宝物
Beloved Treasure

Chapter Twenty-Seven

Dr. David Blackman listened to John Rourke describing the situation and shook his head. "Dr. Rourke, I have no idea how to even advise you on this case. This is certainly unchartered territory. You want me to describe a treatment modality for something no one has ever attempted. We have no vocabulary to even describe the process."

"Doctor, I understand, but this is incredibly important," Rourke said. "I'm thinking it should not be terribly different from reintegrating a subject with multiple personality disorder."

Blackman shook his head, "I disagree; the process would be completely different. By the way, multiple personality disorder has been renamed dissociative identity disorder or DID. MPD, or DID, is defined as a condition in which 'two or more distinct identities or personality states' alternate in controlling the patient's consciousness and behavior. What we have here is an original entity and a duplicate that had no idea he was a duplicate. I don't care how strong a psyche one has; that is going to have some impact."

"I agree with you Dr. Blackman," Rourke said. "However, in the broad view, I assert there are similarities. The most distinctive feature of what you call DID is the formation and emergence of alternate personality states, or 'alters.' Patients experience these alters as distinctive individuals, possessing different names, histories, and personality traits. It is not unusual for DID patients to have alters of different genders, sexual orientations, ages, or nationalities. Some patients have been reported with alters that are not even human; alters have been animals or even aliens from outer space."

"Patients with DID experience gaps in memory, sometimes for long periods of their past and, in some cases, their entire childhood. Most DID patients have amnesia, or 'lose time,' for periods when another personality is 'out.' They may report finding items in their house they can't remember having purchased, finding notes written in different handwriting, or finding other evidence of unexplained activity."

"Another common symptom is depersonalization, when the patient feels his or her body or life is unreal. Some depersonalization promotes a feeling of being outside of their own body, like watching a movie of themselves."

"Okay Rourke," Blackman said, "I see where you're headed, interesting. You're saying the disorder is not alike but the symptoms are, and we should treat the symptoms."

"Exactly, Dr. Blackman," Rourke said. "I knew the original Akiro Kuriname. He was a strong, practiced warrior with a high sense of purpose and honor. Now that we have successfully removed the influence of his creator, the duplicate should manifest the exact same characteristics. Do you agree?"

Blackman thought for a moment, "Yes, I agree provided he is a first generation duplicate and provided his creation was based on the genetic material from the original. Otherwise, each new generation created has errors. It is literally like making a copy of a copy of a copy. The last generation is not as clear or sharp; simply put, the quality is less."

"I believe he is a first generation," Rourke said. "I'm sure he feels as real as you and I do. He is Akiro Kuriname; I'm saying we have to give him the tools he needs to capture his own heritage."

Chapter Twenty-Eight

Paul Rubenstein and his son, Jack, crowded around the computers working on the book, *The Unabridged History of the Rourke Family Adventures*, it was coming along nicely. It was already up to nearly 50,000 words and still only had chronicled a part of the story prior to the Night of The War. Annie and Natalie had left an hour ago driving to Emma Rourke's; the girls had scheduled a day of shopping.

The protective details guarding the Rourke's had reduced after Michael Rourke's rescue from a full 24-hour, 7-day a week rotation of 8 men to a single shift, single person. Harry Livingston, the day shift Secret Service Agent, was monitoring the eight cameras that had been installed for 360 degree coverage of the outside perimeter of Paul's property. Life in the cul-de-sac neighborhood had for all intents and purposes returned to normal.

"Mr. Rubenstein," Livingston said looking up from the monitor screens, "do you have a UPS delivery schedule for today?"

Paul hollered back, "Not scheduled Harry, but I'm expecting a package from Mid-Wake. I didn't think it would arrive before the day after tomorrow. Jose Zima must have found what I was looking for a lot easier than he expected. Why?"

"A truck just pulled up along the curb," Livingston said. "He's backing into the driveway. I'll sign for it."

"Thanks Harry." Then Paul turned to Jack saying, "Son, there is a large cardboard box in the crawl space above the garage marked 'Wildman.' Would you go get it for me?"

"Sure Dad," Jack said and headed to the garage. He dropped the ceiling mounted stairs and climbed up, switching on the lights in the small attic.

Harry Livingston was standing at the open front doors as the UPS truck backed slowly up the drive before making a sharp turn and inexplicably cutting directly across the front yard. "What the hell?" Livingston shouted at the driver, "Get off the grass you idiot!" At that instant, the two double doors at the back of the truck flew open and a green energy blast slammed into Livingston.

The bolt of green lightening blew a hole through Livingston and took out a portion of the wall behind him with a blast of sound almost as loud as thunder.

Paul jumped to his feet and made a lunge for his Schmeisser on a rack above the fireplace. "Hold it Mr. Rubenstein," said a cold voice, and Paul stopped not yet half way to the 9mm sub gun.

"Hands up," the voice said. Paul raised his hands slowly and turned. Two other men entered the front door, stepping over Livingston's body, and began searching the house.

"Who are you, and what do you want?" Rubenstein shouted at the top of his voice. "What the hell are you doing?"

"Who I am is unimportant. What I want is you, and what I'm doing is taking you prisoner," said the man. He stood a little over six feet tall with hard chiseled features. Paul denoted a slight accent in the man's voice. Had this been before the Night of the War, Paul would have been tempted to describe it as Eastern European. The man was well-muscled, clean shaven, and projected an aura that said no-nonsense would be tolerated. "Where are the other members of your family?" he asked after the other two returned. Both shook their heads silently.

"Everybody else left several minutes ago," Paul said. "I'm here alone, except for the agent you just killed; his name was Harry Livingston."

"When will they be back?" the man asked.

"Not for several hours," Paul answered.

"Check the garage," the man ordered. "The garage door was down when we pulled up; see if they are out there."

One of the other two attackers went to the door that lead into the garage from the kitchen and looked. Then, he advanced into the garage to check the other side of the station wagon parked there. Thirty seconds later, he reentered the kitchen and closed and locked the door. "No one is out there; there is only one personnel door at the back of the garage, and it has a latch locked from the inside."

"Damn it," the man said. "We wanted the entire family, but you will have to do."

Paul breathed a sigh of relief; Jack must have realized what was happening and had been able to pull up the stairs. It wasn't much edge, but at least his son was safe for the moment. The leader went to the fireplace and pulled down the Schmeisser, removed the magazine, and after checking the empty chamber, dropped the weapon and magazine on the floor.

"So," Paul said, "what happens now?"

"Bind him," the man ordered. Paul held out his hands in front of him, and zip ties were affixed to his wrists by a man Paul now designated as Number Two. Paul was roughly shoved onto the couch, and his legs were zip tied together at the ankles. The third man searched the rest of the house for more weapons, finding Paul's old Browning and a variety of other weapons. These, he unloaded and discarded. "Now," the man said with a trace of a smile. "Now, we wait."

*****

Tim Shaw had not yet entered his private office when his phone rang. Pulling his cell phone out, he opened it and seeing the number said, "Hello, Jack..." Shaw stopped dead in his tracks then signaled another agent to start a trace and to begin recording the call. Grabbing a tablet and pencil, he asked, "Where are you? Do you know how many? Okay, listen to me; sit tight, right where you are. Turn the ringer off on your phone right now. Don't accept any calls from anyone but me. Sit quietly, and don't move around. Turn the light off in the attic."

Shaw started writing and held up a sheet of paper that said: "Hostage situation Rubenstein's house, agent dead, Paul captured, Jack hiding; roll our team." The office exploded into a flurry of activity.

"Jack," Shaw said, "you are doing very well; I'm proud of you son. Now, give me a few minutes, and I'll call you back. You turned off your ringer? Good. Make sure the light is off, and lay down behind some boxes if you can. Just don't move around more than you have too." I'm hanging up now.

Shaw directed an agent, "I want the full protective details reinstated on the Rourke family. Get on the phone and contact Annie Rubenstein; check the GPS

98

on her cell phone, find out her location, and dispatch a team to her. Emma Rourke and the girls are with her. Let the President know."

He dialed the number for John Rourke, "John, Tim Shaw; we have a problem. Where are you? Good, stay there and stand by the phone—give me five minutes, and I'll call you back." Hanging up before Rourke could even ask a question, Shaw turned back to the agents in the "bull pen."

Shaw sat down, took a deep breath then began barking orders. "I want HPD and County notified now. I want a ring cordon around the area for three blocks in any direction. I want a second ring three blocks out from there and a third one three blocks further out. I want County to set up road blocks on any road that can exit that area. Then, contact the fire department and start evacuating the area, starting with the outermost ring and moving progressively inside. I want eyes in the sky and a patrol boat off the coastline near the house. I want SWAT and the Hostage Rescue Team to establish a command post in the second ring as soon as it is evacuated."

Taking a cigarette from a pack in his shirt pocket, he fished out his lighter and rolled the wheel. It took three tries before he got the cigarette lit; then, he made the call. "John," Shaw said, "Paul has been taken hostage at his home. Jack is hiding in the crawl space attic above the garage. He has a cell phone and got word to me; I told him to turn the ringer off and only accept calls from me. I have one agent down. There are three armed men in the home. I'm cordoning off the entire subdivision, and we'll start evacuating the area in layers from the outside and moving inward. Paul and Jack are alright for now. The rest of the family was not home; I'm sending protective details to cover them. I don't have any other details right now; you know as much as I do."

Shaw listened for a response; it took almost a minute before Rourke answered. "I understand John," Shaw said. "As soon as we have the command post established, I'll let you know its location, and I'll meet you there." Flipping the phone shut, Tim took another drag of the cigarette before crushing it out. Wiping his face slowly with both hands, Shaw quietly said, "Shit" before standing and looking around at the people watching him. "Let's go people!" he shouted clapping his hands together for emphasis. "We have to develop a plan.

I want facts, not your conclusions; 'a conclusion is just the place where you got tired of thinking.'"

*****

Emma's phone squealed in her purse; she saw John's number and answered, "Hey Babe... Yes, we're at the mall." Now, she listened, "Okay, hold on a moment. Annie, could you pull over for a moment?" Annie Rubenstein guided the car into the parking lot. "What?" she asked, trying to get information from Emma.

"I understand John," Emma said and folded the phone closed. Taking a deep breath, she turned to her daughter-in-law, "Annie, there is a problem. All I know right now is that Paul has been taken hostage at your house. Jack has not been, and he is okay for right now. We are to wait here for Secret Service Agents to contact us."

The blood from Annie's face drained, and Natalie and Paula began to cry in the back seat.

Two black SUVs pulled in behind their car, and agents from their protective details they recognized secured the area. "Mrs. Rubenstein, Mrs. Rourke, we have an incident, and I have been instructed to ask you to accompany us to secure location. May I ask you to secure your vehicle, please? Mrs. Rubenstein, would you and your daughter accompany Agent Jones? Mrs. Rourke, I need you and your daughter to accompany us, please."

*****

Within 45 minutes, the outside and second rings of the cordons had been established, and the 140 homes and businesses within them had been evacuated. The Command Post had been set up within two blocks of Paul and Annie Rubenstein's home. It took another 30 minutes to evacuate the inner ring, all without incident. The HPD command trailer, one from the County Sheriff's office and a Secret Service van, were now linked with direct communications, not only to each other but also including fire and city utilities. A no-fly zone had been established, allowing news choppers no closer than one mile from Paul's home.

Two Coast Guard patrol boats had been stationed approximately a mile off the beach located across from the scene and behind a row of homes that completed the south side of the cul-de-sac. John Rourke and Tim Shaw had stepped outside the Secret Service van and were discussing options. Rourke exhaled a long plume of cigar smoke and turned to Shaw, "Tim, I need to know how the protective details were pulled. It's only been six days since we recovered Michael; that seemed a bit early, and now I have to examine whether that was a setup to create this situation."

"John," Shaw said obviously uncomfortable, "I don't know how they were pulled. After Mike's rescue, I think people just assumed the threat was over; but, I'm checking to find out." Rourke started to speak, but Tim held up his hand, "I know, I know. When you assume, it makes an ass out of you and me. John, all I can say is I'm sorry."

Rourke took another drag and said, "Okay, it is what it is. What are we going to do about it?"

"The negotiator is ready to make contact with the house. Let's go back in and see what we're dealing with."

*****

Paul Rubenstein checked the wall clock. Nearly two hours and forty-five minutes had elapsed since the start of this; still, there was no contact from the outside. *I wonder if anybody even knows,* he thought. Then, the phone rang.

The leader motioned for Paul to pick it up, "Put it on speaker, so I can hear both sides of the conversation." Scooting on his butt across the hardwood floor to the coffee table, Paul sat up and, having to use both hands, answered the phone, "Hello."

"Mr. Rubenstein, this is Agent Layne Gretski with the Secret Service; are you alright sir?"

"Yes, I am for the moment."

"Mr. Rubenstein, I have been authorized to tell you that Mrs. Rubenstein, your daughter, and your son are okay. Mrs. Rourke and her daughter are okay as well. Do you understand?"

Thank God, Paul thought, *Jack is okay, and they are in touch with him. Good boy, Jack.* "Yes, I understand."

"Good," Gretski said. "May I speak to whoever is in charge?" Paul held up the handset of the phone to the leader; he smiled and, taking the phone, said, "Yes."

"This is Agent Layne Gretski with the Secret Service; may I ask to whom I speaking with?"

"You may ask, but we both know I'm not going to give you my real name. Why don't you just call me Richard?"

"Very good, Richard how can we resolve this issue?"

"Layne, I'm fully aware of your standard procedures in a situation like this. Understand; I'm not willing to negotiate. The plan is simple. I will tell you what I want; you will give it to me, or Mr. Rubenstein will die. Do you understand?"

"Yes, Richard but surely there is something I can get for you, something to make this a little less stressful. What would that be, Richard?"

"Very good Layne, here's how it is going to work; I do not want to see a chopper, a cop, or anybody. I realize you have evacuated the area; by the way, that was very smooth. I almost did not see anyone; from this point forward, I DON'T WANT TO SEE ANYONE AT ALL. I don't even want to think there might be someone out there. Do you understand?"

"Yes Richard, I can see you probably have more experience at this than I do. I understand, and there will be no one in the area; I give you my word."

"Good Layne, by now, I assume that all I have to do to speak with you is pick up the phone and you will be on the other end, correct?"

"Yes, Richard that is correct."

"Good, then wait until I contact you. By the way, unfortunately, we have one casualty, your agent; Livingston I believe is his name. You may recover his body which is now lying in the front yard. I will allow one ambulance with a driver and attendant. They are to pull in front of the house, parking in the street.

The driver and one attendant may recover the body, load Agent Livingston on a gurney, and place that gurney in the ambulance. They are to continue around the cul-de-sac and immediately leave the area. If there are any deviations from my instructions, I'll kill both of them and leave all of the bodies to rot. Do you understand?"

"Yes Richard, is it acceptable for the ambulance to arrive within the next 15 minutes?"

"Yes Layne, that is acceptable," Richard said and broke the connection.

Chapter Twenty-Nine

"Give me your phone Tim," Rourke said. Shaw handed it to him, and Rourke dialed a number. In a whispered voice, Jack answered, "Hello..."

"Jack, it's Grandpa John. Are you okay?"

"Yes, sir," Jack said in a barely audible whisper. "Is Dad okay?"

"Yes Son, he is. Now listen, after this phone call, I don't want you to speak on the phone; you might be overheard. When we talk again, I'll ask you some questions. You are to turn the light in the attic on and off to answer. One short blink is for yes and a long blink is for no; two short blinks mean you don't know, understand? In a few minutes, there will be an ambulance pulling up. When you see it, wait until the men step out of it then do a short and long blink. Try to keep those same patterns. If we ask for numbers after that, do three short blinks, wait a couple of seconds, and then do the number of blinks needed to answer the question. Do you understand?"

"Yes, Grandpa."

"Good boy, Jack. We'll get you guys out of there; I promise. Now, hang up."

"Love you Grandpa."

"Love you too, Son," Rourke said and handed the phone back to Shaw. "Okay, we have eyes, and we can get some intel as long as we keep it simple." Shaw nodded. He called the ambulance attendant over to where he and Rourke stood. "Yes sir," the young attendant said.

"Okay boy, how well can you fall?" Rourke asked.

"Excuse me sir?"

Shaw handed him a green small device. "This is a video camera. On the front side of the garage facing the street is a small decorative window. When you get out of the ambulance, I want you to slip and fall down. I want you to drive the spike on the camera into the ground so that the camera is pointed at the garage. It has a fish eye lens, so it doesn't have to be perfect. Do you think you can handle that?"

"What's your name son?" Rourke asked.

"It is Dale, Mr. Rourke."

"Dale, my best friend, and my grandson are in that house. I need your help, and you have to be careful; the bad guys will be watching you from the house. If you can't plant this camera without getting caught, forget it; but if you can, it will really help us."

Dale squared his shoulders, "I won't let you down Mr. Rourke; I promise."

*****

Ten minutes later, the ambulance pulled up in front of the house. The driver parked in the middle of the road, not next to the curb. He got out first, pulled the gurney from the back, released the latch, and raised it to its full height. Dale exited on his side, walked to the rear of the ambulance where the driver waited, and together they started moving toward the yard where the blasted body of Agent Harry Livingston lay.

The driver was pushing the gurney with both hands. Dale had his hands fully extended above his head; when he stepped onto the curb, he slipped, falling face down, arms fully in front of him, and unable to catch himself. He laid there for a moment to gather his senses. The driver stopped. Dale pushed up from the ground, stood up, and slowly raised his hands back above his head; together, they retrieved Livingston's body and returned to the ambulance then loaded up and drove off.

"Perfect," Shaw said looking at the video feed. The camera, barely a half-inch in size, was functioning flawlessly, and it was in the correct position. "John, come here and take a look at this." Rourke walked over and smiled.

"Give me that phone again, Tim."

Jack opened the phone but didn't speak; Rourke said, "Excellent Jack; now blink the light once. Very good, I can see it. How many people are in the house?" There were three short blinks then three long ones, "Are you saying three people?" There was one short blink. "Good Jack, are they all in the house?" One short blink. "Are they all in the same room?" Two short blinks, he didn't know. "Are you still okay?" One short blink. "Good boy, I'll call you back in a little while, okay?" One short blink.

Rourke and Shaw met the ambulance as it pulled next to the command center. Dale got out and asked, "Did it work?"

Rourke smiled and clutched Dale's shoulder, "Perfectly," he said. "You did a good job, Dale."

Examining Livingston's body, Shaw said, "Definitely an energy weapon John."

Rourke stepped to the body and peered at the gaping wound in Livingston's chest. "Yes, and I've seen this burn pattern before Tim. This is not the same pattern we saw at the assassination attempt on Michael. The energy output of this weapon is different. Tim, I want Livingston's body to have a full autopsy, and I want the tissue examined closely. I'm talking electron microscope. I want to see the cellular disruption and compare it to reports in the Mid-Wake archives."

"You think you've see this pattern before?" Shaw asked.

Rourke nodded with a concerned frown on his face. "Yes, I believe so. If I'm right, we have just added another player to the game."

"What's your gut telling you John?"

"If I'm right, and analysis will prove it one way or another, this pattern will match a Russian energy blast. That, however, is an issue we will deal with at a later date. Right now, we have to figure out how to get Paul and Jack rescued. Have there been any demands from the hostage takers yet?"

Shaw shook his head, "Agent Gretski, the negotiator, says no. He is waiting for contact from the bad guys."

"Okay," Rourke said after a moment of pondering, "are your teams in position?"

"They are," Shaw said. "However, from the time we give the order to breach the house, getting to the house is the problem. There is too much open ground; it could give the bad guys several seconds to realize the attack is underway and kill Paul as well as themselves."

Chapter Thirty

The phone rang on the coffee table; Richard pushed the speaker button, "Layne, I thought we had agreed that I would call you when I had something to communicate."

"Richard, I'm sorry to deviate from your instructions, but I've just been made aware of a medical condition that Mr. Rubenstein suffers from. I think you need to know about it."

Richard looked at Paul who had appeared to be resting on the floor, slumped to one side for the last several minutes. Richard went to Paul and checked his pulse; Paul stirred. "Okay, Layne, what is this medical condition?"

"Mrs. Rubenstein has just advised me that Mr. Rubenstein takes a prescription medication for a heart condition," Gretski lied, reading the script he had been handed. "He had an episode two days ago, and his doctor has ordered an immediate change in his prescription. Mrs. Rubenstein had gone to the pharmacy to pick it up. I have confirmed this with his cardiologist who said it is imperative the new medicine be administered immediately, or Mr. Rubenstein could suffer a massive and potentially fatal cardiac event within the next several hours. The cardiologist has also requested he be allowed to examine Mr. Rubenstein."

"I'll call you back, Layne," Richard said and disconnected. He stood for a moment, thinking. "What do you say about this Mr. Rubenstein?"

"I did have an event," Paul lied. "I was not feeling well and went in for a checkup. They did an EKG and took some blood. I was told they would let us know something as soon as the reports came in. We got the call this morning from the doctor, and Annie insisted I stay here while she picked up the medication. The doctor, I don't remember his name, Annie dealt with it; he told us I needed to be on the medication as soon as possible and to come back in this evening for an examination."

"Govno!" Richard shouted. Slowly, drawing out the words, he whispered, "Sookin syn," as he wiped one hand over his face. Paul smiled to himself; he had been right about the accent. Govno means "shit" in Russian, and "sookin syn" means "son of a bitch." Switching back to English after taking a series of deep breaths, Richard smiled at Paul.

"Actually Mr. Rubenstein, this improves my situation. The plan called for us securing your family and you. Circumstances, however, prevented that; now, I can increase my number of hostages, while insuring your own good health." Richard punched the speaker button on the telephone again.

"Yes Richard," Gretski answered immediately.

"Okay Layne, as a ... what do you people call it? As a sign of my good faith, you may send the doctor in."

"Thank you Richard; the Doctor asked if it would be permissible to have an assistant also to help examine Mr. Rubenstein should he go into a crisis. I assume this is very stressful for him."

"Sure, why not?" Richard smiled. "The more the merrier but, Layne, no tricks."

"Of course not, I'll call you back and let you know when to expect them," Gretski said and held up a thumb.

Rourke slapped him on the back when Gretski killed the connection and said, "Good job." Turning to Shaw, he said, "Okay, let's get working on this. I think we can get Paul and Jack out of there now. Tim, I need a favor." Grabbing a piece of paper and scribbling a short message, he handed the note to Shaw. "Can you get this message to this man at this address?"

Shaw read the address and note, "Are you thinking what I think you're thinking?"

Rourke nodded, "I am. Get him here, and I mean as soon as possible."

Chapter Thirty-One

Akiro Kuriname had changed into a set of scrubs; Rourke was now wearing scrubs and a long-sleeved white coat. It was the kind traditionally reserved for doctors with the title MD or DO, not the short white coats worn by medical students. Rourke had his hair grayed and, with some minor makeup applied, looked much older. Rourke asked, "Akiro, how's the range of motion in your left arm?"

Kuriname stood and made a series of fast and powerful movements with both arms ending up in a powerful stance. "John, I can do this. Probably not alone but with your help, we can rescue your people." Rourke nodded.

"Then, follow my lead," Rourke said. "We're going to have to improvise a lot."

"What is the plan?" Akiro asked.

"That's what I'm talking about. The only plan we have is to kill or capture the bad guys and rescue Paul and Jack. I don't have a good idea of exactly HOW that we're going to do it. Just be ready, and when I move, you move. Okay, Agent Gretski, make your call. Tell them doctors Johnson and Chu will be arriving within 20 minutes. They will be unarmed, carrying two medical bags and one defibulator, just in case."

Gretski made the call. Eighteen minutes later, a black sedan with County Medical Examiner imprinted on the side pulled up in front of Paul's home. Rourke and Kuriname, in light-blue scrubs and white coats, exited from the back seat with their equipment, and the sedan pulled away, circled the cul-de-sac, and left the area. The "aged" Rourke slowly carried one bag, while the Kuriname had a large medical kit plus a hard case that said "AED" in large letters. As they entered the front porch, the door opened, and they were ordered to place the three containers on the floor and to step back. Complying, they waited as the bags were carried inside and searched.

When they were told to come in, Rourke saw Paul sitting hog-tied on the floor, one armed man watching the back of the house and the second covering the front. Richard stood next to Paul, covering the three of them with an energy rifle. The man from the back of the house came forward, and Rourke and his "assistant" were roughly searched for weapons. Richard, pointing at the AED, said, "Explain this device to me."

Rourke picked up the bag he had carried inside, walked to Paul, and knelt down. Looking up at Richard, he said, "Give me a moment to check my patient." Looking at Paul, he saw a slight smile. Pulling his stethoscope, Rourke began his "examination."

After a moment of checking his vital signs, Rourke turned and told Richard, "I am Doctor Johnson, Mr. Rubenstein's cardiologist. This is my assistant Dr. Chu. The device is a portable heart defibrillator. Should we have an event, it will help restore the natural rhythm of the heart should the patient begin to experience either a dangerous arrhythmia or cardiac arrest."

"It will only be used should the patient suffer an event since the electrical shock they produce can damage a beating heart. This defibrillator sends out an electrical shock roughly 60 to 100 times per minute. As these shocks pass through the sections of the heart, muscles contract and make the heart beat. When a person is in cardiac arrest, time is of the essence. It has a battery inside that carries a charge, but I'd like Dr. Chu to go ahead and plug it into a wall socket just for safety's sake, if that's alright. Mere minutes can be the difference between full recovery, death, or permanent damage."

Richard nodded, and "Dr. Chu" placed the heavy case on the coffee table, pulled a long, heavy extension cord from the case, and plugged one end into the device and the second into the wall. Pulling a blood pressure cuff from the bag, Rourke wrapped it around Paul's upper left arm and pumped it up. Placing the stethoscope on the pulse junction at Paul's elbow, he began slowly releasing the pressure and watching the dial. Rourke frowned and performed the procedure a second time. "I must ask that these restraints be removed; the constrictions and the stress of this situation are causing serious problems with his blood pressure, and I need to administer an injection immediately. Can one of you bring me a glass of water from the kitchen?" No one moved.

Richard said, "Let me see the syringe and the medicine." Rourke handed him the syringe hard case with two syringes, one medicine bottle with pills and two vials of clear liquid. Rourke explained as he placed a thermometer in Paul's mouth, "The first injection will be a thrombolytic; these drugs are also called clot busters. They help dissolve a blood clot that's blocking blood flow to your heart. The earlier you receive a thrombolytic drug following a heart attack, the greater the chance you will survive and lessen the damage to your heart."

"This pill is nitroglycerin which is used to treat chest pain or angina, temporarily opening arterial blood vessels and improving blood flow to and from your heart. Angina, or angina pectoris, is the pain or discomfort that occurs when the heart muscle's demand for oxygen exceeds the supply. Beta blockers, nitrates, or calcium channel blockers may be used to control angina. I know you are experiencing some level of discomfort, are you not Mr. Rubenstein?"

Paul nodded. Rourke continued, "The second injection is of Streptokinase, a protein produced by beta-hemolytic streptococci. It inhibits the tissue destroying machinery of the body. There are two drawbacks for streptokinase therapy; the first is if there has been a previous administration of the drug, I would declare a contraindication for a second because of the risk of anaphylaxis. Secondly, the thrombolytic actions are relatively nonspecific and can result in systemic fibrinolysis. That is the disintegration or dissolution of fibrin, especially by enzymatic action."

"Now about that water," he said looking at Richard, "are you getting it or should I get it myself?"

"Why don't you do that Doctor?" Richard said with a smirk.

"Fine, I shall. May I remove these restraints? I assure you he is in no shape to present a threat to you or anyone right now."

Richard nodded, and Rourke searched the medical bag. "Dr. Chu, excuse me; do you have a pair of scissors in your bag? Mine aren't here, and I don't think this gentleman would be comfortable if I pulled out a scalpel." Chu dug in his bag, handed a pair of long scissors to Rourke, and stepped back. Rourke cut the ties first from Paul's feet and then from his wrists, laid the scissors on the floor, and asked, "Dr. Chu, would you help me sit Mr. Rubenstein up on this footstool." As Paul rubbed feeling back into his wrists, he was sat on the stool. "Now, where do you keep your drinking glasses Mr. Rubenstein?"

Paul answered, "Last cupboard on the left, the small ones are on the top shelf." Rourke locked eyes with Kuriname and winked. Without waiting for permission, Rourke turned to the kitchen, turned on the faucet, and opened the cupboard door. The 'old' doctor made a show of stretching and reaching onto the top shelf, finding what he was seeking. Rourke hollered over his shoulder, "Yes, I found it." Then, Rourke turned and fired a Metalifed four-inch Colt Lawman .357 into the face of the man who had followed him into the kitchen.

Dr. Chu, Akiro Kuriname, exploded into action with a leg sweep that dumped the second man on his ass just before he delivered a crushing stomp to the man's esophagus and launched a spinning kick in the opposite direction that slammed into Richard's weapon. Paul also was in motion, having snatched the long-handled scissors up, driving them into Richard's crotch, and throwing himself to one side out of the blast range of Richard's weapon. Rourke swung around the kitchen door and quick tapped two 158 grain jacketed hollow point rounds, ripping into Richard's face and spraying the room with brains, bone, and blood. Paul jumped up and ran to the garage, pulled down the stairs, and hollered, "Jack!"

Outside, the screech of tires from responding units could be heard. Paul returned with Jack who ran to Rourke. "Grandpa, you did it. You saved us."

Rourke smiled hugging his grandson, "I could not have done it without your Dad and this gentleman. Paul, Jack, this is my friend, Akiro Kuriname." Kuriname bowed.

"I have to ask," Kuriname turned to Rourke. "How did you come up with a gun?"

"I didn't have to come up with it," Rourke said with a smile. "It was already there; I just had to figure out how to get to it."

"Several years ago," Paul said, "John taught me a valuable lesson. Today, it finally was put into play. John was injured in one of the operations, nothing serious but it had him laid up for a while."

"I realized," Rourke said, "I could not defend myself physically. That was a shocking realization for me, and I didn't like it. My mobility was grossly limited for several weeks; Paul helped me position weapons in every room of my house."

Paul said, "John told me he didn't want to be any further away from a gun than two steps and a stumble."

"We have raised our kids around weapons," Rourke continued. "They know how to shoot, and they know the dangers of having live weapons around. They know they can ask to see any weapon, and we'll safe the weapon and answer any questions they may have about the weapon. They also know a loaded gun is a dangerous tool that must be respected; they know a loaded gun can take a life, but they also know it may be the only way to save a life."

"Today, this loaded gun took two lives, but it saved four others," Rourke handed the .357 to Paul. "Looks like you need to clean and reload this, my friend."

Paul said, "Yep, that's about like you John. Come to my house, make a mess I have to clean up, shoot my bullets, and make me clean my own weapon."

Rourke smiled and placed his hand on Rubenstein's shoulder, "Like I've always told you Paul, you have to plan ahead."

Chapter Thirty-Two

Brigadier General Jimmy "J.J." Jones cut an imposing figure, six feet four inches tall and two hundred sixty five pounds of hard muscle with a perpetual five o'clock shadow that extended from his jawline to the top of his shaven head. His starched fatigues accentuated his physique, and while, physically, the picture of the consummate military professional, he was in fact both a traitor and a pervert. However, he was also a cunning bastard who had survived repeated attempted coup d'états and still remained the number two person in the Hawaiian Provincial Guard which had replaced the National Guard after the Night of the War.

Today, he was briefing a combined joint operation of the Provincial Guard, state and county law enforcement agents, and Secret Service Special Agents. Operating under the direct order of Acting President Darkwater, the mission was to "root out enemy agents located within the affected area with extreme prejudice."

Standing at the front of the briefing room in front of a large framed map of the area, he cleared his throat for effect and began, "Gentlemen, satellite imagery has identified this as the site of our operation. Our intelligence reports include a lot of documentation from the early construction diagrams, newspaper accounts, and activity reports of this area during the 20th Century. Historically, this particular area was identified as the Waiāhole Ditch and Tunnel System, and is located on the eastern side of the Waiāhole Forest Reserve area. The system was originally conceived in about 1905 as a way to transport surface water from the wetter windward side of the island to the sugar cane fields on the drier leeward side. It had been abandoned after the Night of the War."

"The main tunnel portion of the system was constructed through the Koolau Mountains from 1913 to 1916. Although it was originally designed to transport surface waters, high level water and dike impounded ground water was encountered during the construction of the tunnel. Between 1925 and 1935, additional tunnels, the Kahana, Waikane #1, Waikane #2, and the Uwau Main Tunnels were developed to collect the high level water. In 1964, the Uwau Tunnel was extended 177 feet past the crest of the Koolau Range. As the system collected more dike water, it collected less surface water."

"The area was damaged and never really functioned again after the Night of the War. Several modernizations were completed over the centuries, utilizing all or some of the original system; when the final changes were finished 70 years ago, it completely bypassed the entire older system which was then totally abandoned."

Tim Shaw stood and raised his hand, "General..."

"Yes, Agent Shaw," Jones said, his irritation at being interrupted clear to everyone in the room.

Shaw plunged on, "What is this system made up of, exactly?"

"Originally, there was a system of ditches as well as tunnels," Jones said. "The entire system consisted of dike water development tunnels, surface water intakes, open ditches, gates, flumes, siphons, roads, trails, camps, support shops, etc. That system started at Kahana Valley in windward O'ahu and collected primarily groundwater and some surface water through a series of tunnels in the Ko'olau Mountains, transporting the non-potable water to Central and Leeward O'ahu primarily for agricultural purposes on about 4,000 acres of sugar cane lands."

"How big is this thing?" Shaw asked.

Jones, now really becoming irritated, said, "If you'll stop interrupting, I'll get to that." Taking a deep breath, Jones continued, "The total length of the Waiāhole Ditch and Tunnel system is approximately 25 miles, stretching from Kahana Valley to the Leeward plains. The system is comprised of two major parts. The collection part of the system consisted almost entirely of tunnels, starting from Kahana and running through Waiawa. This is where the water is collected. At Waikane, there are two development tunnels: Waikane One Development Tunnel and Waikane Two Development Tunnel. The system then enters the lands of Uwau and Waianu. Here, the Uwau Development Tunnel has two components: the original Uwau Tunnel on the windward side of the Koolau crest and its extension on the leeward side of the Koolau crest."

"Beyond the North Portal, the system-wide tunnel then goes downstream, descending and entering into the lands of the Waiawa; it is also known as the

Waiāhole Main Bore. The length of the system is about 14,500 feet, and the elevation is approximately 724 feet at the south portal and 754 feet at the North Portal. I also need to caution you that the Trans-Ko'olau Tunnel or the Waiāhole Main Bore develops groundwater. The entire system runs from the northwest of the Kahana valley, along the Ko'olau Mountain Range, to the southeast and the Waiāhole valley with the side tunnels entering the main system at these points." Jones drew the bayonet from his side and pointed; he always liked the impact that had.

Clearing his throat again, Jones boomed, "Now, on to team assignments. Secret Service, you will hit Waikane #1 and #2. The Honolulu County Sheriff's Department will cover the Kahana and North Portal routes, and that will leave Provincial Guard personnel to hit the Uwau Tunnel, its extension and the Trans-Ko'olau Tunnel. Bear in mind, these systems have been abandoned for a long time; there is no telling what obstacles you may run into. It is possible that entire sections have collapsed and are impassable; it is almost a certainty that we will encounter hostile forces. We will have attack helicopters and fighter jet support from the Kaneohe Marine Air Base."

Jones saw a hand come up in the back but could not see who it was attached too. "Yes, in the back. Please stand and identify yourself."

The man stood and asked, "What type of weaponry will be employed?"

Jones' frustration betrayed itself again, "I said to 'stand and identify yourself.' Who the hell are you?"

"My name is John Rourke, General, and I'm trying to determine how many of these people you're going to get killed in this operation, that's all."

"We will be using the standard energy type weapons we always use, why?"

Rourke shook his head, "That's what I figured you would say. General, those weapons will not work on these opponents. I've come up against these forces twice; I guarantee you they won't work." Pulling one of the Detonics from his shoulder holster, Rourke said, "You need weapons like this to win against them. I assume, General; your plan is to win. Correct?"

Chapter Thirty-Three

Transport of the various teams to their assigned locations had been accomplished by both ground and air transports. The process of transport had begun at 0230 hours. The Honolulu County Sheriff personnel had been formed into two teams. Team One was to enter the Kahana tunnel at 0430 hours; they had moved into their assigned area via the highway that ran from the old Schofield Barracks location to Whitmore Village.

They were to clear the entrance and move to the main tunnel and, if no resistance was encountered, move southward to make contact with the other teams and continue to sweep the main tunnel. The second Sheriff's team had been flown by chopper from Highway 63 to their location at the south end of the tunnel system to "catch any rats leaving the trap."

The two Secret Service Teams had offloaded with the first Sheriff team and, utilizing their AATVs, had moved to their locations. Tim Shaw and John Anders were leading the two Secret Service Teams that would be exploring Waikane tunnels #1 and #2. They were to have Shaw's team enter Tunnel #1, clear the entrance, and begin moving south to hook up with Anders where the entrance for #2 connected to the main tunnel. Five minutes after Shaw started into Tunnel #1, Anders and his team would start on #2. Should resistance be found in #1, it would be possible to plug that hole with Anders' team.

Failing to find resistance, Shaw would join forces with Anders and the Sheriff's personnel, and all teams would continue to move southward toward the other tunnels and the teams that would be entering them at staggered times. Within 30 minutes of Shaw's entry, all other teams should have entered their tunnels and plugged the hole trapping any enemy combatants.

The Provincial Guard had driven from Pearl City as far as they could then moved out on foot to get to their locations. General Jones had divided the Provincial Guard personnel into two teams. The first team, led by Jones, had entered the Uwau Tunnel and its extension. The second team, led by Major Chris Barnett, was in the Trans-Ko'olau Tunnel. Barnett was an excellent officer, a strong leader who took care of his people, while taking care of the mission; the exact opposite of his narcissistic commanding officer. By 0330 hours, all teams were in position and ready.

In the final minutes before the push was to start, each of all of the team's members were making final checks on their weapons. John Rourke, with Tim Shaw's team, heard one of the Secret Service Agents intone what could be his last prayer, "Lord, make me fast and accurate. Let my aim be true and my hand faster than those who seek to destroy me. Grant me victory over my foes and those who wish to do harm to me and mine. Let my last thought not be, 'If only I had my gun,' and Lord, if today really is the day you call me home, let me die in a pile of empty brass."

At 0410 hours, the attack helicopters from the Kaneohe Marine Air Base launched for the short flight to the tunnel system. Ten minutes later, the fighter jet support launched from the same base and established a high-level CAP (Combat Air Patrol) flight pattern of the tunnels. For the ensuing 20 minutes, everyone waited.

All of the personnel involved in the Tunnel Sweep were dressed in black military-style energy suits, complete with helmets that offered secure communications and infrared sight modes. Four men from each team comprised the lead search elements; they were armed with energy rifles but carried pistols with conventional ammunition. The rest of the teams carried the Lancer M-16 A-12s, which used standard lead and copper nickel slugs.

John Thomas Rourke had insisted on this based on his first encounter with Captain Dodd at the Mediterranean archeological site and the Battle of the Forest. John carried his standard CAR-15, his twin Detonics .45, and the Magna-Ported and Metalifed Colt .357 Python at the small of his back.

The hard chrome plating process that Metalife perfected had some remarkable properties compared to traditional chrome plating. Metalife's hard chrome plating would not separate from the base metal. The superior bond eliminated flaking and cracking seen with traditional hard chrome. Critical edges, sharp edges, and threaded edges weren't affected by the chrome plating nor were critical tolerances, as the standard thickness ranged from only .00005" to .0005".

Knowing the energy weapons would not work against the clones and their energy suits, Rourke's hope was the use of those energy weapons by the American forces would make the enemy more aggressive and the non-energy weapons would save the day.

Sheriff Royce Crawford made a final call to his second team and confirmed they were ready to make entry. Six years ago, Crawford had been the youngest Sheriff ever elected for Honolulu County. At six feet four inches tall and weighing in at 245 pounds, he was now a seasoned veteran of law enforcement. Early in his second term, he had created a Special Response Team; today was their first actual mission other than training.

Crawford knew that he had to secure the northern end of the tunnel system; that would involve entering the eastern tunnel access opening and making his way to the main tunnel, leaving a holding force there and splitting off a team to turn north and clear the northern tunnel access. Once that had been accomplished, that team would rejoin Crawford, and they would begin the sweep southward to hook up with the other "friendlies."

Each of the teams had difficulty locating the entries to their access tunnels due to the active or adaptive counter-illumination camouflage. It had taken each team about 10 minutes to locate the entries and pass through that barrier.

The Secret Service and Provincial Guard units were to hold positions where their access tunnel joined the main one. This way, at every access junction, more personnel would be added to the sweeping force as it headed down the main tunnel; the only questions were what kind of shape were these tunnels in and when would they contact the enemy?

Arriving at the junction, Sheriff Crawford sent 10 men north, and 20 minutes later, they returned without enemy contact. Crawford started his rejoined force down the main tunnel; the operation was now fully engaged.

John Rourke and Tim Shaw's team had been forced to scramble over fallen debris from the roof on the Waikane access tunnel. Dirt and rocks had nearly filled the tunnel in two places; while it was obvious the roof could collapse at any time, they carefully negotiated past the obstacles and in 20 minutes were at the junction with the main tunnel; they waited. John Anders' team found their access tunnel wide open. Their tunnel floor was dry, and they were able to move into position at their junction in about 10 minutes; they waited.

General "J.J." Jones had immediately run into trouble in the Uwau access tunnel. Forty feet in, the entire roof had given way at some time and completely blocked the tunnel. He sent a squad to begin trying to dig through at the top of the cave in. Twenty minutes of digging had gotten them nowhere, and Jones, "eager for an opportunity to join the fight and garner some glory," ordered two explosive charges set to clear the debris and moved his men back to just inside the opening of the tunnel.

When the charges detonated, more of the roof came down, and on the outside slope above the mouth of the access tunnel, the vibrations set off a landslide that effectively covered the opening. Jones and his team were sealed in, which was in accordance with The General's revised plan. His original plan had been to lead his men into an ambush; he had alerted Captain Dodd of the plan, and the American forces would have walked into a trap.

Because of Rourke's involvement, Jones had decided instead to simply take his people and himself out of the battle and let the chips fall where they might. By the time his men were able to dig out, the battle would be over and Jones would be one step further along in his overall master plan.

Major Barnett had the largest force, over 200 men and heavy weapons. He had established a secure perimeter around the Trans-Ko'olau tunnel and its two extensions. He had sent half of the force to the western tunnel and the other half to secure the southern and eastern access portals. There, he was joined by the second County Sheriff's team. Their primary job was to cover the exits and engage any of the enemy forces that were flushed out of the tunnels by those entering higher up on the tunnel system.

Chapter Thirty-Four

Sheriff Crawford's team moved tactically down the tunnel toward Rourke's position. The tunnel was mostly, but not completely, straight. Clearing the next section around a twist or turn required care and caution. Hooking up with Rourke and Shaw's team had occurred on schedule. John Rourke was now in the lead and had advanced about 10 yards when he felt the explosion and dropped immediately to his one knee. He watched as loose debris rained down from the ceiling and sides of the tunnel.

"What the hell was that?" Tim Shaw asked in a whisper after kneeling next to Rourke.

"I don't know," Rourke said drawing a bead down the tunnel in the direction they had been moving. "Let's just stand by here for a minute." Holding up a clenched fist, Rourke signaled a stop.

Crawford came up to him and whispered, "Contact?"

Rourke shook his head, "Don't think so, but let's hold here for a minute or two and see what happens." Once inside the tunnel, the communications within their helmets were not penetrating the rocks above them. The other teams were holding position inside their access tunnels, and none of them could talk to the other teams.

Crawford motioned two of his men to come forward and whispered, "Take a look; we'll cover you." With a nod, they advanced to a left-hand turn in the tunnel. While the man on the right "sliced the pie," the one on the left side knelt to provide low cover.

Rourke watched with a critical eye, while remembering the old CIA Weapons Instructor who had taught him how to slice the pie, something he had passed on to his children. "Start as close to the wall as possible, without scraping up against the wall. Make sure you are at least an arm's length away from the corner. You don't want your arm to stick out into the doorway. Observe the corner, and keep in your mind that the pivot point will be the apex of the corner."

"Take a small step 90° away from the wall. This is the start of a semicircle you will make around the corner. Keep your elbows in and your front foot parallel to your line of sight so that neither gives you away."

"Pause and scan the slice of the pie. Between each step taken, you should scan from the floor at the corner to ceiling, scanning each slice in a vertical manner. With a firm, two-handed grip on your firearm, lean slightly toward the direction you are stepping to allow your head and your eyes to be the furthest object—this allows you to see your target before he sees you."

"If you are proficient with both hands, use whichever hand that will keep you most concealed. Never cross your feet. This is a very unstable position, and if something or someone hits you or you are forced to shoot midstride, you'll be in trouble. Instead, move your lead foot, the one in the direction which you are stepping; then, follow with your trailing foot. Also, be aware of your feet; make sure you are not pointing your toes into the corner, as they may precede your eyes, which means the suspect may be able to see you before you see him."

"Practice by setting up a mirror in the room. As you are slicing the pie, check to see what you can see in the mirror. Try to adjust your form so that little more than your eye and your firearm are visible. You can also practice with another person using flashlights. As soon as one of you sees any part of the other, shine your flashlight on them. The competitive nature of this drill will sharpen your form quickly."

"Always point your firearm where your eyes are looking. This will allow you to react more quickly than if you have your firearm at low ready. Arms extended or high-compressed ready are both good options. With high-compressed ready, make sure your non-firing hand is behind the plane of the muzzle."

"Remember the 'fatal funnel.' The 'fatal funnel,' as it is affectionately known, is one of the most dangerous areas to be in when traversing a building. This area includes doorways and other portals which only allow a narrow area in and out of a room, like narrow hallways and archways. If you were picking a choke point for an ambush, fatal funnels would be perfect places to focus your attention."

"It is in your best interest to spend as little time as possible in these areas. At a doorway, the fatal funnel is the area on either side of the door, as deep as the door is tall and just as wide. Since standing to the side of a door does not count, obviously the fatal funnel is an imaginary area—an area which the bad guy might not respect, so just because you are out of the fatal funnel doesn't mean you can't be shot." It amazed Rourke that, in over 650 years since he had first learned it, the technique was still being taught.

Chapter Thirty-Five

A Marine Sergeant came up to the Vice President with a note and whispered in his ear. Darkwater turned his head toward the ceiling, closed his eyes for a moment, and then said, "Let her in." The sergeant went back to his post and opened the door.

Natalia Tiemerovna-Rourke, former Major in the Russian KGB and now America's First Lady, walked into the oval office followed by her protective detail. The lead on the detail had locked eyes with Darkwater and held his hands up in helplessness. Darkwater nodded his understanding and moved to intercept Natalia. The First Lady was dressed in a formfitting black dress with boots. She wasn't happy. Five of the six men in the detail lined the walls of the presidential office; the sixth one went to the window and faced outside watching the grounds.

"Jason," Natalia said without prelude, "we need to talk."

"Natalia, how is the President?" Darkwater asked.

"That's what we need to talk about," Natalia said. "For your information, Michael is fine. In fact, under normal situations, he would be here right now. But, these are not normal situations, and I need to discuss a plan with you."

"Is this the way you want to do it?" Darkwater asked and motioned toward her protective detail. "Or, should this be a 'you and me' conversation?"

"No, we need to do it this way," she said, and she unceremoniously plopped down on the large couch and crossed her long legs. If you accept this plan, it needs to be handled as a top secret operation. However, I want witnesses. Jason, it is not that Michael and I don't trust you; having said that, there are 'elements' in this administration that we do not trust."

"Lay it out then," Darkwater said and sat across from her.

"Jason, simply put," Natalia said, "while the rescue mission to find Michael was being launched, some of our operatives came to me with information. As a result of that information, when it was found, we have commandeered the floor of the hospital that Michael is on. Michael is no longer in the hospital, and his medical status has not been released, except to some very select individuals; these are primarily my protection detail."

"Unfortunately, we have discovered there is a conspiracy that threatens not only this administration but also the country, and we fear the rest of the world. We have traitors in our midst," Natalia continued. "Michael and I have spoken about that possibility before, but it was just supposition."

Darkwater frowned. "I take it you now have proof?" At a wave of Natalia's hand, Secret Service Agent Matt Songren, her protection detail leader, stepped forward with an envelope and handed it to the Acting President. Darkwater pried open the metal clasps, inverted the envelope, and pulled several 8x10 photographs out. They were obviously surveillance photos. They showed Phillip Greene exiting a vehicle and approaching the front of an office building.

The others showed several other "well-placed" politicians doing the same, but it was the last two pictures that startled the Acting President. The first showed Captain Dodd exiting the same office building. The date stamps showed the pictures to be in sequence, covering a period of two hours. The last showed Brigadier James Jones standing in a parking lot with Captain Dodd and Phillip Greene.

"Holy shit!" Darkwater exclaimed; then remembered his position and clearing his throat, he said, "You have total faith in the validity of these photos?"

Natalia nodded, "Holy shit is correct, and yes, I do, Mr. Acting President. I shot them myself as witnessed by Secret Service Agent Matt Songren. Agent Songren, are you able to verify my statement?" Songren simply nodded to Darkwater. Darkwater stood and began pacing.

"What unholy alliance have these people constructed?"

"We don't know for sure, but we have our suspicions," Natalia said. "Let me play this out for you. First, we know without exception that the real Captain Dodd died a long time ago. This is now the third time we have seen his face the past months. Second, we know those Captain Dodds are in fact clones of the original working with an alien force identified by The Keeper as the ones responsible for the devastation of the planet and the human race some 40,000 years ago. We have incontrovertible proof that force has returned, although we still don't know what their agenda is. Lastly, we have the former presidential candidate from the Progressive Party, several high ranking members of that party, and the number two man in the Hawaiian Provincial Guard consorting. What is your opinion, Jason?"

"This is worse than even Michael and I imagined," Darkwater said. "What can I do?"

"First of all, ensure there are no leaks on Michael's status," Natalia said. "It is public knowledge that he was located and recovered, but don't release any more information than that; you could, however, let it leak out that Michael's not ready to resume the office of President. We need the public and the Progressives to believe you have assumed his duties."

"Are you sure Michael is on board with this?" Darkwater asked. "I'll do it, but I need to hear it from him."

The man standing behind the Acting President left his post by the window. Facing the Acting President for the first time and looking up, "You're hearing it from me right now Jason." Darkwater turned and looked into the face of Michael Rourke, President of the United States.

"We need surveillance on all of these people, and I don't want to go to the normal organizations; I'm thinking you probably still have some contacts with Naval Intelligence," Rourke said. "Can we do this totally off the board through them?"

Darkwater stood up immediately and crossed to Rourke, extending his hand, "Mr. President, damn Michael it is good to see you. How do you feel?"

"I'm fine Jason; now, can we do this totally off the board with your intel folks or not?"

Darkwater recovered from his initial shock, sat back down, and wiped his face. "Yes Mr. President, I can make this happen."

Rourke smiled, "Then, make it so Admiral. Make it so."

"So, what exactly is your plan?" Darkwater asked.

Michael Rourke sat down next to Natalia. "I need to have 'complications' that keep me out of the public eye until we have these people identified and ready to be rounded up. First of all, when we do move, I need to have absolutely incontrovertible proof of the allegations. Secondly, we need to identify how Dodd, this Dodd, came to be here and what ties exist with his alien masters.

Thirdly, we have got to know what the alien plan actually is and how they plan to implement it. That could be an international concern."

Darkwater frowned, "What do you mean international?"

Natalia spoke up, "Jason, long before the Night of the War, my former country was heavily engaged in UFO research. It was because of Russian intervention that my father-in-law did not recover a UFO that had crashed in Canada. A Russian scientist named Doctor Vassily Batrudinov interrupted John at the site, and the craft and its pilot were destroyed in the explosion."

"Batrudinov survived that encounter and went on to continue publishing scientific articles in which he stated emphatically that his belief in extraterrestrial visitation was unshakeable. He claimed, however, that to his knowledge no physical evidence had ever been found, at least not by the Soviet Union. I know that was a lie," she continued. "During my activities with the KGB, I repeatedly saw evidence that had been recovered from sites in Siberia and several states belonging to the Union of Soviet Socialist Republics."

Darkwater stood and began pacing again, "You believe that Russia may be aligned with the aliens?"

"I don't know Jason," Michael said. "Maybe they aren't, in which case we have one issue; but if they are, that's a whole other ball game, and we need to find that out. By my estimates, we need to find that out, right now."

Darkwater nodded, "So, back to your plan; what is it?"

"Primarily two phases," Michael said. "Phase One, we need a cover story that says I'm being moved to the Presidential Retreat for some kind of medical rehabilitation and I'm currently unable to continue actively in the presidency but expect to be fully recovered in a couple of months. As far as Phase Two goes, I want you to stay on in the role of Acting President, and I need you to hand pick personnel from your days at the Office of Naval Intelligence. I'll leave the choice of personnel up to you. They need the resources of the ONI, but I have no problem if your people are retired agents as long as you personally can vouch for them. I want the traitor identified, and I don't want them to even smell somebody is on to them; any ideas?"

Nodding, Darkwater said, "Yes sir, I do."

"Good Jason," Rourke said. "We'll be leaving now. You're points of contact with me will be limited to Natalia and my father. There are to be no reports over the phone or other electronic methods. Face-to-face and only at a specified location that you will be advised of. Jason, we don't have a lot of time. We're sitting on a couple of potential powder kegs and a national scandal."

Darkwater stood and shook hands with the President, "I understand Michael; thank you for your trust in me. Now, get out of here, and let me get started."

Darkwater returned to the desk as the entourage exited and picked up the phone, "I need the Press Secretary in my office as soon as possible." Then, he dialed another number. When the connection was made, the only response was several short beeps followed by a long tone. When that ended, there was silence. Darkwater said one word, "Lockout" and broke the connection.

Chapter Thirty-Six

Contact with the enemy came as it always does: sudden, explosive, and deadly. The teams coming from the north end of the tunnels had negotiated several twists and turns. Rourke estimated they had cleared approximately two-thirds of the overall length of the tunnel. As the point team rotated, the fresh team made a turn to the right and rounded a final obstacle of mounded debris. That was when three of them, Sheriff Crawford's men, were cut down by green blasts of energy.

The lone survivor threw himself backwards, rolled back behind the debris, and began firing his energy rifle down the tunnel toward the threat. Chunks of rock and dirt exploded from the pile, and one energy blast after another sizzled into it; the survivor was forced to retreat back the way he came.

"Okay, we have contact," he said into his helmet speaker. "I think I'm hit and I'm falling back." As the bulk of the teams moved forward to engage, Shaw pulled six men out of the rush and told them to provide rear security. Visibility was dropping quickly, the vibrations were causing small cascades from the ceiling and walls of the tunnel, and the energy blasts were literally melting dirt and rock; the resulting smoke was acrid and irritating. Luckily, their helmet filters kept most of it out of their lungs, but the smell still penetrated.

Using the wall, a barrage of energy blasts were directed by Shaw's men toward the enemy to keep them engaged while the rest of the teams got into position. Shaw waved for one of his men and shouted, "Get into position on the left, and fire at will."

Two men crawled to a firing position; one carried a long barrel heavy weapon that reminded Rourke of the old Barrett .50 caliber semi. However, instead of the 12.7x99mm NATO or .50 BMG ammunition originally developed for and used in M2 Browning machine guns, nicknamed the Ma Deuce, this weapon carried a box magazine filled with a caseless exploding rocket round similar to a small RPG or Rocket Propelled Grenade.

The round was almost the same size as the .50 BMG round just slightly larger, and it did not have the range of the Ma Deuce. However, the nearly

1,000 grain projectile not only had the massive destructive power of the original round, but it had the advantage of being able to be set for impact or proximity detonation. A twist of the nose of the round determined which was to be used. The first five rounds were sent down range within 3.5 seconds, and as the shooter dropped the empty magazine, his assistant gunner handed him another.

The first five rounds had been suppressive fire set for proximity detonation, as were the next five. Then, the gunner switched to impact rounds and began laying down slow and deadly fire. Return fire from the enemy slowed but did not stop; from this point forward, it would be pretty much a stalemate.

Anders and the Sheriff's second team could hear the battle sounds coming from the mouth of the tunnel. Anders took his three squads forward into the tunnel leaving the Sheriff's deputies as security. Once inside, he rigged a series of anti-personnel mines to catch escaping bad guys, if they got past his team. They could be triggered remotely to fire simultaneously or individually by breaking a beam.

The squads would drop off as they came to each of the side tunnels, carefully clearing each one and returning to form up together before proceeding. Anders reasoned that whatever enemy forces were positioned in front of him now would be trapped between the teams moving in from the north and his group moving from the south; they were effectively blocking inside the tunnel. The question was could the good guys keep the bad guys bottled up and that would only be answered by firepower, training, and luck.

*****

John Thomas Rourke, the agents and deputies were slugging it out inch by inch down the tunnel. Fortunately, it seemed to him they were making headway, and so far, their casualties had been relatively light. The energy suits his people were wearing could not totally protect them from direct hits, but they were able to dissipate a significant amount of energy from anything other than those direct, square-on energy impacts.

They had already moved past the point of the initial contact and had discovered their own ammunition had effectively penetrated the suits of the enemy.

130

So far, the body count totaled 28 enemy dead and 16 wounded. His own losses were eight dead and a handful of pretty significant burns. If the percentages held, Rourke felt pretty positive about the outcome. Suddenly, all return fire from the enemy ceased.

Sheriff Crawford and Shaw ordered a cease-fire. The tunnel was suddenly extremely quiet, except for the whimpers of the wounded. "May I request a temporary truce?" a voice from the other side shouted. Rourke looked at Crawford and Shaw, "What do you think guys?" Sheriff Crawford hollered back, "Okay, let's all take a breather!" He whispered, "Be ready for anything folks; this can all go to hell again in a heartbeat." Five minutes went by with no further contact.

The same voice shouted from the darkness, "I would like to speak with whoever is in charge; is that possible?"

Crawford shouted back, "Exactly how do you want to do that?"

"I will lay down my weapon; I have ordered my people to stand ready but not to fire unless I order it. Can we meet in the middle between our two forces?"

Crawford turned to Shaw and Rourke, "What do you think guys?"

Rourke said, "I'll do it if you want me to. I think you two need to stay here with your people should that heartbeat come." Shaw and Crawford looked at each other; it made sense. "Okay, John," Shaw said, "but be careful."

"I'm coming out," Rourke shouted. "When I see you, we both start walking, but understand if you try anything, I promise my people will cut you down in your tracks."

"That is acceptable."

Rourke peered deeply into the darkness until he saw movement. He handed his CAR-15 to Shaw and said, "Hold this for me a minute." Then, he stepped out and moved forward as his opponent started walking toward him. Rourke silently counted 48 paces; about 20 still separated him from his enemy. "That's about far enough," Rourke said. The man stopped and began to unbuckle his helmet. Rourke saw the face of Captain Dodd emerge. *I'm really getting tire of this guy,* Rourke thought and removed his own helmet. "What do you want to talk about Captain Dodd?"

Dodd looked puzzled, "You know my name?"

"Let's just say I am acquainted with you," Rourke said as he ripped the wrapper from a cigar and palmed his lighter. "Although you are probably not aware of it," Rourke said, "your family and I have some degree of history."

Dodd studied Rourke's face for a full 30 seconds, "Ah, yes. I believe you are Dr. John Thomas Rourke; are you not?"

Rourke blew a smoke ring and replied, "Guilty as charged." Then, he shifted his weight in case he had to grab the .357 Python from the small of his back. "What's on your mind, Captain Dodd?"

"It appears sir that we are at a stalemate, Dr. Rourke. The sensors we have throughout this tunnel indicate there is a secondary force approaching from the other end. That makes the current situation... untenable shall we say. What are your terms for surrender?"

Rourke's face never changed as he took another drag on the cigar before exhaling forcibly. "Terms of surrender? There are no terms Captain. If you wish to end this, surrender will be immediate and unconditional. If you want to continue this little get together, likewise your deaths will be immediate and unconditional. It's your choice."

"May I have a moment to discuss this with my people?"

Rourke shook his head, "No sir, you may not. Surrender now, order your people to drop their weapons, put both hands over their heads, and file toward us in single file. Otherwise..." Rourke left the message open.

"You drive a hard bargain, Dr. Rourke."

"Understand Captain Dodd, we are not bargaining. You asked a couple of simple questions, and I have given you a couple of very simple answers," Rourke took another puff and slowly let it out. He pulled off one of his gloves and slid the cuff of his energy suit up a couple of inches. Looking at the Rolex on his left wrist, Rourke simply said, "You have 30 seconds to give me your answer starting... now."

Dodd stared at him for a full 20 seconds without an answer. Rourke started counting, "10, 9, 8, 7..."

"I accept your terms, Dr. Rourke."

Rourke nodded, took another puff, and said simply, "Wise decision Captain. Now, order your men to do what I said to do. When you have done that, you are to raise your own hands and start walking toward my men."

Dodd turned and gave the orders and instructions. The sound of scrapes from weapon butts being grounded and movement began to fill the tunnel. Sheriff Crawford ordered a team of deputies forward, "Frisk them and cuff them." Shaw ordered his agents to assist.

A total of 30 men walked forward, were searched and cuffed, then were ordered to sit along the wall of the tunnel. Six more wounded were found unarmed as Crawford's people moved forward. They were searched and secured; then, three deputies began administering first aid. Shaw personally had control of Captain Dodd.

Sheriff Crawford walked up to Rourke, "Hey, do you have another one of those cigars?"

"I didn't know you smoked Sheriff," Rourke said as he handed a cigar, pulled his lighter, and spun the wheel.

The flames illumination lit both of their faces, "Used to, I think I just started again. Thanks John. You're a pretty cool character under fire. If you ever consider law enforcement as a career, call me."

Rourke laughed, "Sheriff, do you have any idea how long I've been trying to retire? Thanks for the offer anyway."

Agent Billings, lead element of Ander's force, shouted out, "Hello, what is your status?"

Crawford shouted back, "Come on in; everything is over with, and we are secure!"

Billings shouted back, "The sign is 'Earth!'"

Crawford shouted, "The counter-sign is 'Shine,' come on in!"

Anders came out of the dark and scanned the scene, "It looks like you boys have the situation in hand."

Rourke nodded, "How did you guys do?"

Anders removed his helmet and said, "We took some fire but looks like the main battle line was here with you."

Rourke nodded, "Can you get word out your end of the tunnel? We probably need to send a runner; the helmet radios are only functional for short distances and line of vision in here."

Anders sent one of his men to contact the outside word. "You got a minute John? I've got something to show you and my boss."

Rourke nodded and hollered, "Shaw, come here!" When Shaw walked up, he said simply, "Anders, are your people all okay?"

Anders nodded, "Yeah Boss, thanks for asking. I've got something you need to see." Turning, he led the two back the way he had come from. A hundred yards down the tunnel, they saw a tarp hanging from one wall. Anders approached and grabbed one end, pulling the tarp back. Inside was a small cave that appeared to be freshly dug, and sitting in the middle of it on three legs was something that took Shaw's breath away.

Shaw smiled and said, "Is that what I think it is?"

Rourke nodded, "Yes sir, Mr. Shaw. That is a real life unidentified flying object. I suspect that this is the missing UFO from the attack on the presidential inauguration. Evidently, Dodd or one of his people piloted it here."

Shaw patted Anders on the shoulder, "Good job John. Just wait until the science geeks get their hands on this little baby; any idea how we'll get it out of here?"

"Yeah, you remember that damn thing we have been tripping over all day?" Rourke said kicking at the ancient narrow gage railroad tracks at their feet. "We'll roll it out on these."

Chapter Thirty-Seven

The Navy missile cruiser, USS Dagger, was plowing the waters from Oahu to Mid-Wake ostensibly returning Dr. Williams following his meeting with the Under Secretary of Commerce, Dillon Hooper. Acting President Darkwater had arranged for himself and several "guests" to make the trip; it was all an elaborate ruse to conduct a super-secret meeting of Lockout.

During his last assignment with the Office of Naval Intelligence, Lockout had been the brainstorm of the then sitting president, President Michael Franklin. He was beginning to see undercurrents forming in his administration that were, in his words, problematic. He foresaw a potential for a time in the future were there would be a need to "circumvent the system." Lockout had been established as a method to accomplish exactly that.

Neither President Franklin nor the two Chief Executives who had followed had been required to activate it, but the process had been kept in place. It was known only to the President and the Lockout Team which consisted of individuals specifically chosen for their commitment to the country and their positions within the scientific and intelligence communities. Over the years, the individual team members had been shuffled due to retirement, death, or assignment changes. The selection criteria, however, had remained as stringent as it was on day one.

Down in the Dagger's Officer's Ward Room, the participants were gathered around a long table. Dr. Williams began the meeting, "The Chaos Theory has been described as a 'field of study in mathematics, with applications in several disciplines including physics, engineering, biology, and philosophy. Chaos theory studies the behavior of systems that are highly sensitive to initial conditions, an effect which is popularly referred to as the butterfly effect.' In 1972, Dr. Edward Lorenz wrote a paper entitled *Predictability: Does the Flap of a Butterfly's Wings in Brazil set off a Tornado in Texas?*"

Jason Darkwater took the floor, "In other words, every incident and every happening has the potential for dynamic effects, both positive and negative, throughout the universe. In fact, most of the time, we are not privileged to see those affects because they may not occur in our geographical locations or within our sensory perceptions. In other words, sometimes 'shit happens,' and we don't know why. We are gathered here today to evaluate situations that cannot be discussed outside of this room. Let me make this clear to each of you; this is a matter of the utmost national importance. To say this 'meeting never took place' can only be described as an understatement."

The group was comprised of retired Captains and flag officers as well as Dr. Williams. Retired Captain Jack Shilling was the former head of the Nimitz Operational Intelligence Center. NOIC executed the Office of Naval Intelligence's responsibility for Maritime Domain Awareness (MDA) and Global Maritime Intelligence Integration (GMII). It provided the timely, relevant, and predictive intelligence to all fleet elements, including Maritime Operational Centers.

Retired Rear Admiral Hank Sanders was the immediate past head of the Farragut Technical Analysis Center. His job was to coordinate intelligence activities that would anticipate and analyze rapidly accelerating foreign scientific and technological research, development, and proliferation with the goal of maintaining technological superiority as well as preventing technological surprise. Its intelligence products enable U.S. planning and research and help guide future defense acquisitions.

The Kennedy Irregular Warfare Center had been commanded by Captain Derek Billings until two years ago. They delivered analytical and operational support capabilities to Navy Special Warfare and Navy Expeditionary Combat Command forces engaged globally. They had state-of-the-art, all-source, reach-back capabilities as well as forward-deploying services to support the operational requirements of irregular warfare.

Retired Captain Daniel Thomas Hasher had headed up operations at the Hopper Information Services Center. He oversaw the production of information technology and enabled the rapid and reliable delivery of ONI's intelligence products to service components worldwide.

Darkwater passed out folders to each of the participants, "Here's the deal gentlemen; I believe that each of you will recognize the folks pictured here."

Hasher let out a low whistle and said, "You have got to be kidding."

Darkwater shook his head, "No Captain Hasher, I'm not. And, this is extremely relevant to you personally because of your allegiance to the Progressive Party."

Hasher looked up stunned, "Sir, I hope you understand. I'm an American first and a Progressive second. We can agree to disagree on policies, but I hope you are not questioning my loyalty to this country."

"Dan," Darkwater firmly grasped Hasher's shoulder and said, "if I had any questions about you, you would not be sitting here. I think this will go a long way in showing each of you the delicateness of this situation. This investigation cannot be allowed to go down the path of partisanship and turn into a witch hunt. I believe that decisive action, decisive and immediate action, is on the horizon. The very fabric of this country's political processes are about to be strained, and we have to be careful and professional. Now, I will need to know your best recommendations on how to proceed, and I'm going to need the best from your operational components."

"The primary operational functions from this point forward are critical. We cannot afford mistakes or missteps. We need data, and that data has to be garnered from a variety of sources and triple verified before we can move or, even for that matter, determine how we are going to move. And, understand this; before we move, the decisions that we are going to move and what those movements shall entail must be approved by you as a group. That approval must also be that each and every one of you is in absolute agreement with those courses of action. There will be no exceptions, and no one can simply vote 'present.' As of right now, we are all in this boat, for better or worse; we will sink or swim together. Anymore questions? Then, let's begin."

"Before we get too far down this rabbit trail, Mr. President," Derek Billings said, "I have some concerns." Darkwater leaned back and directed his old friend to continue. "Let me get an understanding; you are saying that it is predictably probable we have a serious breach in national security, correct?" Darkwater nodded. "You are also saying that, if this body agrees, it is also predictably probable some sort of armed interventions will be required, correct?" Darkwater nodded. "Because of the predictable probability, I submit we better consider right now where to get the manpower for that potential eventuality. I do not subscribe we base our actions or potential actions on the concept of using existing forces to accomplish our mission."

"Derek," Darkwater said, "I agree with you 100 percent. The very concept by which Lockout was conceived dictates we have to go outside the box. This, should action actually be required, will have to remain completely off of everyone's radar until, and I say again—if, we are forced to launch any type of aggressive mission."

"From what we suspect right now, we have to consider that the Russians are somehow involved; we just don't know how right now. Second, it appears we have possibly identified some manner of traitorous conspiracy that involves the clones, but we have no idea exactly who is involved or how wide spread it may be. We don't know what the traitors are planning, so the only intelligent path is to investigate. The really tricky part is that the investigation has to remain absolutely secret. If our suspicions are correct..." Darkwater let the sentence hang in the air for a long moment, "we could find ourselves on the verge of a war with two fronts; that is what we have to try to avoid at all costs. I just don't know that we can."

Chapter Thirty-Eight

Following the tunnel sweep operations, there had been a flurry of events both in and around the entire Waiāhole Forest Reserve area. The majority of activity dealt with the ditch and tunnel system on the eastern side. Major Barnett's forces, the Provincial Guard, assisted by Army Pathfinders and two Recon Marine Teams from the Kaneohe Marine Air Base, continued sweeps throughout the entire area. They were looking for stragglers and checking if there were any other potential outposts that had been established by the alien and clone coalition.

Army Combat Engineers had focused on clearing the cave-in debris from the tunnel system and repairing the ancient rail system inside. This was in preparations of removing the alien craft Anders and his team had discovered during the battle.

A total of 42 enemy combatants had survived the tunnel sweep operation; eight of these had subsequently died of their wounds. The eight remaining injured had been transferred to a secure ward at the Tripler Army Medical Hospital in Honolulu; 28 uninjured prisoners had been confined at the new Ambrose Federal Detention Center, near the Honolulu International Airport. Part of the maximum security federal prison system, the AFDC, named for former state Senator Malcolm Ambrose, was under the operational control of the Federal Bureau of Prisons, a division of the United States Department of Justice.

The uninjured had been divided into three groups of nine prisoners and placed in separate cell blocks. The 28th prisoner, Captain Dodd, had been placed in solitary confinement; all were under 24-hour a day electronic and video monitoring.

*****

Tripler Army Medical Center, named after the legendary American Civil War Medic, Brigadier General Chares Stuart Tripler, was in its 15th iteration.

Originally established in 1907 as simple wooden structures within Fort Shafter, it was now ultra-modern and the largest military hospital in the entire Pacific Rim region, its closest rival being Mid-Wake which did not have the floor space.

Dr. David Blackman, Chief of Psychological Research at Mid-Wake; and Dr. Henry Drake, Chief of Medicine at Tripler, turned when John Rourke entered Drake's office. "Good morning gentlemen," Rourke said. "Have you made any headway yet?"

Blackburn stood, "Morning John, I was just briefing Dr. Drake on our experiences with Lt. Kuriname."

"I've seen the reports," Drake said. "To be honest, we still do not understand the method by which the connections between these men and who, or whatever, created them works."

"I don't either," said Rourke. "The Dodd clone we captured before was simply 'turned off,' and I don't know how; apparently, my theory that it was tied to the tattoo was accurate since we have been able to reconnect with Kuriname."

"And, there have been no indicators that he is still in some kind of link?" Drake asked.

"None," said Blackburn. "I suspect that, when Kuriname was knocked unconscious, the link was temporally broken, and since the tattoo was removed prior to his regaining consciousness, it has been severed completely."

Drake frowned, "But if your hypothesis is correct, why haven't these men been 'turned off' as you say?"

"I think that as long as the link is functional," Rourke said, "there is some degree of two-way communication going on. Their creators maintain control of the cloned individuals and are able to use their sensory awareness to gather information. It is like they are passive monitors of everything that they see and hear. Gentlemen, I think we have been 'bugged.' I think the aliens are monitoring what the clones are aware of. My question is what, if anything, can or should we do about it?"

"I believe that Dr. Drake can answer the first part of that. Is there anything that we can do?" Blackman asked.

"I believe so. Since we already have them in custody, we do what you did with Kuriname. Render them unconscious, and while they are out, remove the tattoos. If we are correct, we'll be able to find out in very short order. My concern is that, if their creators become aware of what we are attempting, they will simply 'turn off' all of them at once."

"I agree," Rourke said. "Let's look at the eight injured men first; do you expect each of them to make a full recovery?"

Drake nodded, "We have a couple that are touch and go. Honestly, I'm not sure why they are still alive; six, however, should make a complete recovery. Yet, as a physician, I cannot and will not be a party to using these men as guinea pigs or test subjects. No experiments, period."

"Dr. Drake," Rourke said, "let me explain this to you. If we do nothing, none of these men will ever again see the light of day as free citizens. It will be imperative they spend the rest of their natural lives incarcerated. During the rest of their natural lives, they will remain in communication with a force whose desires appear to be the annihilation or subjugation of mankind. If you will remember your Latin, the root for annihilation is the word 'nihil'; its literal translation is to 'make into nothing,' and subjugation is a verb which means to 'bring under domination or control, especially by conquest.' I don't see that they, or we, have much of a choice here."

Drake removed his glasses and sat them on the desk, as he squeezed his eyes tightly shut. Leaning over, he placed his face into his cupped hands, rocking slowly for a long moment before sitting back up and replacing his glasses, "Okay, I get it. Now, how do we do it?"

*****

Back at the ditch and tunnel system, the recovered alien aircraft had not been nearly as big a problem to move as was initially anticipated. Finally, it was determined the only way to remove the craft without damage was to lift it. That required a gantry to be erected over it; the design and construction was complicated by the fact there was a near total lack of clearance around it. That had taken the most time; once the design criteria had been worked out, it had only taken two days before the gantry spanned the length of the craft and held a system of simple pulleys and ropes.

These were linked to small diameter, high tensile, strength pipes that formed the framework of the gantry. Heavy lifting straps were slung under the craft, raising high enough to roll a wheeled dolly under it. Once loaded, a dozen strong backs moved it forward to the rail tracks. The gantry was repositioned, the entire load was raised, and the wheels lowered into place on the tracks.

Twenty minutes later, everything had been loaded on the bed of a large military truck, covered by a heavy tarpaulin, and was traveling to the coast under heavy military escort. A flight of six attack helicopters from the Kaneohe Marine Air Base flew air cover the entire route. Two fighter jets flew Combat Air Patrol over the harbor, while the aircraft was to be loaded on one of the Navy's largest submersible aircraft carriers for transport and study at Mid-Wake. The trip took one hour; and an hour later, the carrier was steaming toward Mid-Wake. Once it was in deep water, the monster ship slipped quietly under the waves of the Pacific.

The hope was that examination of the craft would give an understanding both of how it operated and flew but also the technology, weapons, and avionics it possessed. As far as the military knew, only one person understood the craft and how to operate it; but, he was in solitary confinement and not likely to divulge that information.

Chapter Thirty-Nine

Jack Shilling, former head of the Nimitz Operational Intelligence Center, and Hank Sanders had taken the initial lead on surveillance and how to gather the field HUMINT or Human Intelligence. HUMIT is simply intelligence gathered by means of interpersonal contact as opposed to other methods. These could include signal intelligence, imagery intelligence, or MASINT or measurement and signature intelligence.

"HUMIT was tricky," Shilling had said. "It is not as objective or as reliable as the other methods; it has to be evaluated because many of the wide variety of sources are of doubtful reliability. It has to be rated for the reliability of sources and the likely or unlikely accuracy of the information they provide. Such information can only be classified as accurate and true if it is confirmed by a number of sources. Sources of that information might be neutral, friendly, or hostile, and may or may not be conscious or 'witting' of their involvement in the collection of information. 'Witting' is the art form of intelligence gathering that shows a person is not only aware of a fact or piece of information but also aware of its connection to intelligence gathering activities."

Dan Hasher's team was involved with the "technical" aspects of all forms of electronic and systems surveillance; he had the "hacker squad." Their jobs were to penetrate computer security, data bases, and any form of communications medium with targeted probes using key words and phrases that had been chosen to show linkages between specific individuals, organizations, and threats. They took those "hits," and these were used to have a starting point for surveillance activities for targeted individuals and groups.

It would be the job of these three men and retired Admiral Hank Sanders to look at, analyze, and evaluate the evidence; and if consensus on an action plan was arrived at, to make recommendations to Jason Darkwater.

At that point, emphasis would shift to Derek Billings as the action arm of Lockout. His people, as yet unidentified, would have to have the requisite special warfare and combat skill necessary to accomplish this mission. He had assigned the task of putting this group together to Marine Chief Warrant Officer

2nd Class, Wesley Adam Sanderson. Sanderson, formerly an enlisted Marine, had fast-tracked through special operations and irregular special warfare training, quickly climbing the ranks. As a Staff Sergeant, he had applied for the Chief Warrant Officer program and shifted from ground operations to military intelligence.

Sanderson's warriors would, if necessary, be the ones who either interdicted operations or took down the specific targets identified by the efforts of the rest of Lockout. During a meeting, three days after the initiation of Lockout, Billings told Chief Sanderson, "You will have control of the hunter-killer teams, if we have to use them. At the present, there are no officers we have identified who will be assigned to you. Wes, you have to understand these teams, if they are deployed, it will have to be without the knowledge or agreement of the current heads of the five individual components of the Office of Naval Intelligence. That deployment can only be accomplished by the direct order of the Commander-in-Chief, Acting President Jason Darkwater."

What none of rest of the Lockout Team realized was that the order would only be coming by direct order of President Michael Rourke through Darkwater. Rourke was still "officially" rehabilitating from several "minor" injuries and exposure he had suffered during his attempted kidnap, or assassination, attempt. Unofficially, he was behind the scenes coordinating access of information linkages for the Lockout Team.

Today, he was awaiting an informal, unofficial "state visit" from the President and First Lady of New Germany, his mother, and her husband, Wolfgang Mann. The entire Rourke clan, including Sarah's grandchildren, was eagerly awaiting their arrival. The missing member was his father, John. John Rourke had declined the invitation saying, "This is your mother's time, and I don't want to interfere or take any time away from her visit."

Chapter Forty

During the first meeting with the KI representatives, The Keeper had told John Rourke, "The society of the KI could best be understood, in human terms, as a constitutional monarchy." Although that description is not completely accurate or complete, within that monarchy were four main categories of citizenship. The being known as The Keeper represented those focused on intellect, philosophy, and free will.

The governing class, The Keeper explained to Rourke, was complicated. "The last living descendant of our original royal line is our leader, but some within my people are, at least passively, advocating for him to either step down or go away. Legitimately, he is what you would call the titular ruler or head of my people. At some time soon, that is going to have to happen. He is aged and not in the best of health; additionally, he has no offspring to continue his family line."

"Upon his death, resignation, or removal, our culture will be forced into a new political system for the first time in generations. Also, while he is in the official position of leadership, he possesses few, if any, actual powers. He does, however, have a following that is loyal to him and much of his exercised power comes as a result of his personality and experience."

The second group was more militaristic in their philosophy. The Keeper had told Rourke that "... many of my people consider that Earth was theirs, and they wish to reclaim it. They have no wish to destroy humanity, although some elements within the KI are far from benevolent. They consider the Earth to be their inheritance and view modern man as interlopers, little more than what you would call squatters. They remember your ancestors as primitive, and there exists certain... biases against all things that are not KI."

The KI that had introduced himself as "The Captain" was the leader of this faction, and his orientation could be described as a "nationalist." According to The Keeper, The Captain's focus is on the spirit or aspirations common to the whole of his people, his devotion and loyalty to his own people; in human terms, he could be described as having excessive patriotism. He is also rather "chauvinistic" in his attitudes because of his biases against all things not KI. His is almost a rabid desire for the advancement, independence, and autonomy of the KI to be in the position as rightful rulers of the Earth. He could be called primordial in his beliefs about the origin and that only one set of ethnic, cultural, and religious beliefs or identity should exist in a single state with other ethnic peoples, cultures, religions, or identities being subordinate to the KI."

In the months since John Thomas Rourke had last seen The Keeper, the sage had been traveling among the smaller European tribes; and from the feedback Rourke had been receiving, The Keeper had been busy sharing his view of Earthly reality with many different and varied cultures. The stories he had heard were that The Keeper's perspective was being presented as a probable direction for the evolution of human civilization.

The Keeper was due back from his trip this evening and had made an appointment to see John. He had asked for the meeting before he made a visit to the New Germany Capital the following month. When his escort vehicle pulled up in front of Rourke's home, John walked over and opened the vehicle door, extending his hand. "Hello my friend," The Keeper said. "I trust all is well with you?"

"Yes," John said. "As always, things are a little tense, but the family is well. Come on in; you said you had something to discuss." As they walked up the drive, Rourke noticed The Keeper's complexion was darker than he remembered; he seemed stronger and younger somehow, as he carried a large case by its handle.

"So, how was your experience with the Tribes?" John asked. "Do you see why we sometimes call them the Wild Tribes?"

The Keeper sat the case on the floor between them and replied, "I did see different cultural norms amongst the people I visited. Remember that in the years I have existed I have encountered not only many Earthly cultures but also many different cultures that you would call Alien. Although all expressed themselves in many different ways, remember that there is a commonality in that all are pieces of consciousness manifest in a physical dimension where they are creating and co-creating their personal realities."

Rourke was stunned. "Do you mean that there is commonness between all incarnated beings, even if they are on other worlds?"

"There are more similarities than differences," replied The Keeper. "It does not matter if they are on other worlds or in other dimensions. The principal difference is the perceived level of separation in physical reality."

The Keeper continued, "Now, remember that all statements about how reality is created have a certain truth to them. All are equally valid. In my experience in this life, I have tried to learn about as many different ways that consciousness perceives reality as possible. I have found certain 'truths or beliefs' to exist or overlap in many systems. I have studied all that I could and then constructed a perception of reality that includes as many as possible, without bringing in some of the more fringe or fragmented beliefs that, although fine for some, are not suitable for my purposes here and now. I will admit to having a certain scientific bent to my perceptions, but I attempt to incorporate all spiritual and scientific beliefs I can. I find that, unless conflicted by certain dogmas, most spiritual and scientific beliefs intertwine."

He continued, "I will share a basic outline of how I find reality to be constructed. First off, there is, and only can be, One… Source, Creator, God, Mind, Reality, or whatever you call the Creative Source/Force of All That Is. Any reality that has a fragmented Source that manifests itself in varying levels of ability or in opposite energies, such as negative and positive, are subsets of the One. This Source is made of Light and consists solely of Light."

The Keeper paused for a moment and then said, "Now, here is where describing Creation, which is actually beyond words, by using words becomes difficult. Words, by nature, have limits, and their understanding is further compounded by each individual's understanding or definition of each word. The meaning that each word has to each person varies; having said that, let me attempt this."

"Reality or life is actually a fragmenting of the Source, which is Light. This Light actually flickers on and off, in and out, out and back, or from nothing to something and back to nothing; all at the same time. There is always perfect balance in Creation. It can be seen when Creation is seen from a clear perspective. 'All That Is' is constructed from this balanced set of actions and is by its very nature digital, at its core always vacillating between the two states. This was first glimpsed by the physicists in the early 20th Century with the advent of Quantum Physics but was not properly understood until the advent of the digital computer age and further understandings in physics."

"Reality is a sort of hologram but is never seen as such due to the nature of the programming. This programming is necessary to maintain the illusion of separateness. It allows the Reality Construct to be useful as a learning tool for developing consciousness, which is another term for … us." Once again, The Keeper paused for a moment and then added, "As your Albert Einstein said over 600 years ago, 'Reality is merely an illusion, albeit a very persistent one.'"

"Yes, I've heard that quote before. What does it really mean to you?" John Rourke asked.

The Keeper replied, "It tells me that no matter how far or how much our science develops and what 'truths' we become aware of, especially at the subatomic scale, that our conscious perception of reality will continue to be guided by the senses and how their data is filtered by our brain. It appears there is a reason for these perceptions, and it also appears that they will continue in this vein for at least some time into the future, if not forever."

"At the basic level, there are two driving forces that manifest themselves in our consciousness construct, entropy, and evolution." He continued, "The inherent drive towards evolution is what allows us to develop or raise our consciousness and, in doing so, makes it more efficient. The inherent drive towards entropy is what removes crystallized thought and creations and allows new creation to begin. To give you a mental picture, imagine there is a spot of ground that was just left uncovered by a retreating glacier. There are soil, rocks, water, and air. All left in that state will eventually break down even more. This is entropy. Put a plant seed into this equation, and suddenly, the items are being used and organized in a different manner; the growth of a plant is part of the equation. The soil, rocks, water, and air are being used in a manner that is a more developed, or evolved, goal. This is Evolution."

"When we, as entities, do not attempt to work with our state of consciousness and develop it to a higher or more evolved level, then we become part of the entropy. Entropy eventually manifests itself as complete decay. Evolution and entropy are just the two vacillations of the Light. They are occurring simultaneously and consistently, and they always have and always will. The only variances are from our slowed down perception of All That Is." At this The Keeper stopped speaking for a moment and seemed to be searching for how—or perhaps—what words to use in continuing his current talk.

"There are consistencies between all consciousness," he said, "whether they be self-aware or not. In the interplay of physical reality, the vacillations of All That Is are passed along by each piece of consciousness. The speed at which this occurs in physical reality is consistent and is measured by the speed of light. To oversimplify, imagine a string of humans changing from facing right to facing left. As each person moves, it signals the next person to change. If you had about 186,000 miles of people lined up, all would complete one move every second. That is the speed of creation in the physically manifest world."

The Keeper went on, "Now, you may wonder why I speak about such things when they seem to be meaningless to the day-to-day reality of a normal human being. I speak of them because, to me, an understanding of life is truly incomplete if a person does not have some understanding, or inkling, of the interplay that occurs just beyond the perception of our five senses. The true wonder of Creation is much more easily brought to mind when you have this awareness underlying the inherent beauty and majesty that is recognized by your senses."

Rourke interrupted The Keeper, "Tell me more about this concept of life being a type of digital reality construct. All I can bring to mind is a bunch of youths playing some video games."

"Before, as you would say, we go down that path John, I have some things I need you to take a look at," The Keeper said. "During my last visit with one of the European tribal councils, I was given these." The Keeper reached down and sat the case on the coffee table. "John, I have concerns about what I'm about to share with you; I need your assurances of confidentiality."

Rourke frowned and stopped The Keeper as he began to open the case, "Depending on what you're talking about, I would say certainly. However, you must understand my position. If what you are about to share has implications that could impact my people or this planet, I can make no such guarantee ahead of time."

The Keeper looked at Rourke for a long moment, slowly dropped his head, and gazed at the floor. "I understand John," he finally said. "While I cannot be sure what these items mean, I fear they will fall into that category. I accept your conditions. Instead of confidentiality, may I count instead on your discretion and ask for your understanding and cooperation if what I suspect is borne out by your investigation?"

"That I can agree to my friend," Rourke said with a nod.

"Here is the first," The Keeper pulled what appeared to be the lower receiver from an energy rifle. It appeared to have exploded; it looked more like a melted glob of twisted metal and plastic than anything.

"Where did you get this?" Rourke asked.

"The leader of a small clan gave this to me," The Keeper said. "This was found at the scene of a massacre of some of his people. As best as he could determine, an entire family had been murdered. His people live in small family units consisting of two or three families co-located in small, isolated settlements you would not even describe as villages."

Rourke was examining the melted blog, "It appears right here there is a primitive hand knapped arrowhead imbedded in the material."

"You are correct," The Keeper said. "His people evidently fought back but were outnumbered, and their weapons no match for their attackers. Here is something else." He placed an earthen jar on the table and pried off the lid; it had been sealed by what appeared to be beeswax. He upended the container and shook something out on the table.

Rourke picked it up, "Crap, is this a human hand?"

The Keeper nodded, "I believe so."

The hand was desiccated, hard and brittle. It appeared to be the right hand of a small human, possibly an adolescent severed at the wrist joint. The wound appeared to Rourke to have been caused by a blast of intense energy and heat. Frozen within the hand was what appeared to be all that was left of a small knife; the hand napped blade was broken off; what remained of the handle appeared to be bone.

Slowly, The Keeper removed a small piece of cloth from his robe. "This also was found at the scene. John, this cloth I believe was made by my people."

Rourke studied the items closely, then he looked at the old sage; suddenly, he appeared even older to Rourke. "Alright my friend," Rourke said, "I need you to tell me what you believe this means."

"John," The Keeper finally sat down heavily on the sofa, "if I am correct, I fear that when that village was attacked it appears that one of my people was present, although I cannot imagine in what capacity. However, I fear my speculations on that subject give me no peace or solitude; however, there is no other explanation for how this piece of cloth could be present."

Pointing at the melted glob he continued, "I am not familiar with this type of weapon; I do know that this was not created by KI technology. So, I have several disjointed pieces of evidence that when taken individually are open to all manners of interpretation; taken collectively however, they present a potential scenario that is completely unacceptable to me and, by virtue of that, my culture."

Rourke stood and began walking; he unconsciously pulled one of his thin black cigars from his pocket and lit it. After a couple of moments, he turned, "What do you want from me?"

"John," The Keeper said, "I am requesting two things. First, can you have these items analyzed and determine if our visual observations are in fact accurate? Second, if they are, I need to be made aware of those findings before any actions are taken by you or your people. This could potentially have devastating consequences for my people."

Rourke nodded, "Here is my suggestion; you need to be present when these items are examined. They need to stay in your possession; you must maintain a chain of custody. Secondly, you need to accompany me. We'll take these items to a friend of mine at the Mid-Wake facility. He will be able to give us confirmation that either your fears are baseless or they are well-founded in scientific proof. Do your people know where you are?"

"No John, I have not contacted them since I came into possession of these items. As far as they are concerned, I'm probably still on my 'fool's errand' of contact with the primitives."

"Okay, let me make a phone call. We need to leave now; do you have any other clothing? You can't travel in your robes and expect not to be noticed."

The Keeper smiled, "I have anticipated you, my friend. I requested a change of clothes recently from your people, and they obliged me; give me a moment to change." Rourke showed him to the bedroom and closed the door. Rourke dialed a number, spoke urgently into the phone, and broke the connection a few moments later just as The Keeper came out of the bedroom. Where a robed sage had entered the room, a white-haired and bearded man wearing slacks, a sports shirt, and light jacket exited. "What do you think?" he asked.

"Hang on; you're going to need a hat or cap to cover that white hair," Rourke said. The Keeper went back into the bedroom and returned after a few moments. His white hair had been piled on top of his head and covered by what appeared to be an English bowler hat from before the Night of the War. Rourke gave a little chuckle and sat, "You look a little like Sebastian Cabot."

The Keeper's face had a quizzical expression; he had no idea who Sebastian Cabot was. "Never mind," Rourke said, "you look great. Let's wait outside; our ride should be pulling up any moment."

Chapter Forty-One

Dr. Fred Williams, head of the Mid-Wake Research Institute, was in town for a scientific conference at the university when John called; William gave Rourke directions and said, "There will be a pass for you and your friend at the gate. Lucky for you, I have the equipment with me."

Rourke introduced The Keeper and presented the materials to Williams; his assistant had carried them to a laboratory. Two hours later, Williams had sent a runner to the cafeteria where they had been told to wait and directed them to a large amphitheater style room.

Williams said, "John, as you know, a Directed Energy Weapon emits energy; in other words, it does not have a projectile. A DEW is capable of transferring energy onto a target with a desired effect that can be either non-lethal or lethal."

Rourke nodded, "Am I correct that energy can be generated in several various forms, such as electromagnet radiation as in lasers or masers? Or particles with mass, as in a particle beam weapon or even sound, like in sonic weapons?"

"You are," Williams acknowledged. "In the old days, they called such weapons death rays or ray guns, and they were treated as science fiction. They were supposedly capable of projecting energy at a person or object to kill or destroy. From the early beginnings of laser development, laser research was focused on the discovery of new wavelength bands, maximum average output power to reach maximum peak pulse energy and maximum peak pulse power. It was also necessary to define the minimum and maximum output pulse duration and maximum power efficiency to optimize such weapons for maximum performance goals."

Williams explained, "All of this began in 1953 when Charles Hard Townes and two graduate students were able to produce the very first microwave amplifier. That device operated on similar principles to the laser but amplified microwave radiation rather than infrared or visible radiation. However, Townes' maser, as he called it, was incapable of continuous output. At the same time, two Russian scientists in the old Soviet Union, Nikolay Basov and

Aleksandr Prokhorov, were independently working on the quantum oscillator and solved the problem of continuous-output systems by using more than two energy levels."

"A scientific report from that time said, 'That enabled them to release stimulated emissions between an excited state and a lower excited state rather than a ground state. That facilitated the maintenance of a 'population inversion' making such a weapon both functional and deadly. By 1955, Prokhorov and Basov were suggesting optical pumping of a multi-level system as a method for obtaining the population inversion; later it was used as a main method of laser pumping.'"

"I think it was in 1964," said Williams, "that Townes and the two Russian scientists shared the Nobel Prize in Physics 'for fundamental work in the field of quantum electronics, which has led to the construction of oscillators and amplifiers based on the maser–laser principle.'"

Rourke turned to Williams and said, "Under the direction of the old Soviet KGB, the peaceful application of the maser-laser principle was discarded for the rapid development of portable and deadly aggressive energy weapons which they perfected after the Night of the War and I've seen in action."

Williams nodded, "To make a long story shorter, these tissue samples bare the signature of the Russian weapons. We also found some genetic material on that piece of cloth, and we have been able to extract some DNA. Unfortunately, while it is very similar to human DNA, it does not match exactly anything in our databases." Producing a swab, Williams turned to The Keeper and said, "Sir, with your permission, I'd like to get a sample from you for comparison; would you please open your mouth and allow me to swab the inside of your cheek?"

The Keeper opened his mouth, and Williams ran the swab up and down the inside of his mouth. Withdrawing the swab, Williams handed it to a technician and said, "Run it right now, and bring me the results." He told Rourke, "This will just take a couple of minutes to get a comparison. The DNA from the hand is definitely human."

Then, he added, "There is something else. This was something that initially was not relevant to your investigation; I suspect now that it might be." He flipped a switch, and a giant view screen came to life. After pushing a series of buttons, he found the specific graphic he wanted.

He said, "There is a field of study called paleomagnetic research. By developing a record of past configurations of the geomagnetic field, we can extrapolate spatial variations of the present geomagnetic field over the globe and time variations of the recent geomagnetic field. By those extrapolations, we can find anomalies."

John shook his head, "I'm sorry Doc, but I don't understand a damn thing you just said."

"Try this," Williams said. "We look for fluctuations that identify something that should not be there, but the fluctuations say it is. Here is the anomaly you're looking for. It is in the Aleutian Trench beneath the Arctic Ice Cap. That trench extends for 3,400 km from a triple junction in the west with the Ulakhan Fault and the northern end of the Kuril-Kamchatka Trench to a junction with the northern end of the Queen Charlotte Fault system in the east. The Aleutian Trench is a convergent plate boundary. The trench forms part of the boundary between two tectonic plates."

"Right here," he said as he highlighted a point on the map. "Right here is what we believe to be your target." Switching graphics again, he continued. "Here is the connection, we think, the Kamchatka Peninsula. It is a 780 mile Russian peninsula with an area of about 100,000 square miles between the Pacific Ocean to the east and the Sea of Okhotsk to the west."

"Okay, Doc," Rourke said. "What does all of that mean?"

"Based on some very spotty intel, this could be where the resurgence of the 'Russian' influence is based. I believe we have discovered the location of a second Mid-Wake type facility they built back before the Night of the War; if I'm accurate, it could very well mean their threat is back; and I hypothesis, based on this conversation, things could be complicated by a direct involvement with the KI."

"You're saying the KI are aligned with the Russians?" Rourke said. "Why?"

"I don't know, John," Williams said. "I can't say that they are. What I'm telling you is that the evidence is indicating it. Where else would the KI have gotten this technology, and more importantly, how else would a KI have been in possession of this weapon?"

The technician returned and handed Williams a sheet of paper. Williams scanned it, pushed his glasses on top of his head, and handed the report to Rourke. "Gentlemen, as you can see, we have a match with the sample we took from the piece of cloth you brought me. That DNA matches the sample we took from you sir." The Keeper nodded, "However, it does not match your own DNA but is from someone who shares your bloodline. DNA from Homo sapiens does not possess the distinctive markers that are present in your DNA."

"To be exact, DNA from humans and DNA from your people appear to be exactly the same for 99.3 percent of the markers. That is to be expected since the planet of your origin was Earth and the physical similarities between our peoples indicate a shared genetic history, probably resulting in a common ancestor in both of our pasts. However, it is that last seventh-tenth of one percent that clinches the fact that the DNA recovered from the cloth is definitely from a member of the KI."

The Keeper nodded and turned away; when he faced back to John Thomas Rourke, the pain was evident in the old man's face. He took a deep breath and said slowly, "My friend, this confirms my worst fears. This is a situation now that presents serious and deadly consequences for both of our peoples; this is a crisis the like of which my people have not experienced for tens of thousands of your years. I am at a loss to describe, or even contemplate, the next move."

Rourke noticed a single tear roll gently down the wrinkled face of the old sage. It was a face that now looked older and more strained than Rourke had ever seen. The anguish of the truth played across his entire demeanor. The Keeper felt, for the first time in a long time, the sheer agony of loss and absolute dejection. "Someone, one of my own people, has taken steps that are beyond my capacity to understand, steps that would irrevocably alter my people and yours for all time."

"Alright, we need to proceed carefully then," Rourke said. As they walked out of Dr. Williams' office, Rourke could feel the weight of the crushing sensations The Keeper was experiencing; they emanated from his very being like waves of negative images, images that Rourke saw in his own mind almost like a telepathic kaleidoscope running wild; he had never experienced such a sensation. While they impacted Rourke's mind's eye, he could not comprehend the images of devastation and destruction.

"John," The Keeper finally spoke as they approached their car, "I must return to your home and change back into my robes. I must go back to my people immediately."

"I would suggest that you stay here," Rourke said with concern. "I don't know if it's safe for you to return."

"No," The Keeper said firmly. "There are many questions that I must find the answers for and the only place I can get those answers is up there." He vaguely pointed toward the sky. "I do not comprehend what is happening, but it is imperative that I get those answers now. Can you arrange for the authorities to contact my people and ask for transport for me?"

"Certainly," Rourke said, "if you are sure this is what you want to do."

"It is not what I want to do, John. It is what I must do."

Arriving back to Rourke's home, The Keeper changed, while John made the phone call. Twenty-five minutes later, they stood at the airport waiting for the KI transport. A small craft, the size of a small bus, streaked into sight and hovered in front of them. It extended three landing skids and settled on the tarmac; a panel opened and stairs came down. The Keeper stopped when the shuttle pilot appeared at the hatch. The pilot was armed with a pistol of some type on his left hip.

The sight shook The Keeper to his core, "Thank you John," he said and climbed the stairs. The stairs withdrew, and the hatch was closed; moments later, the craft disappeared into the sky. The sight of the pistol had not escaped John Thomas Rourke's gaze; a sense of dread settled over him. He recognized that weapon. He had seen its type before, only that time he had been facing down the barrel of it. Rourke had killed the Russian Spetsnaz officer who had been about to fire it at him. Silently, Rourke wondered if he would ever see the old sage again.

Chapter Forty-Two

The two worse injured detainees were removed from the medical ward for "transfer to the ICU." In actuality, they were simply placed in a smaller, secure medical ward; their current status made it too dangerous to attempt the excisional biopsy procedure. Two hours later, on schedule with the administering of their "evening meds," the other six were simply "slipped a Mickey" in the form of a powerful and quick-acting sedative.

Each was transferred to a gurney and rolled into an operating room where an anesthesiologist put them all of the way under; the tattooed tissue was removed, a layer of synthetic skin was applied, and the wound was bandaged. In less than 24 hours, the Syn-skin would be integrated with the tissue below it and would appear like the normal skin grafts of regular human tissue.

Syn-skin is a kind of artificial skin made from shark cartilage and collagen from cowhide. The mixture is dried and sterilized to make a thin membrane similar to the human dermis layer. Next, a protective top layer of silicone that acts like the human epidermis is applied. This patch acts like a framework onto which new skin tissue and blood vessels could grow. The only drawback is those new cells never produce hair follicles or sweat glands, which normally form in the dermis.

As the new skin grows, the cowhide and shark substances from the artificial skin breaks down and are absorbed by the body. Decades earlier, the first application of Syn-skin had been used on a woman whose burns covered over half her body. After peeling away the burned tissue, a layer of artificial skin had been grafted on some of her own unburned skin. Three weeks later, the woman's new skin, the same color as her unburned skin, was growing at an amazingly healthy rate.

*****

The process at the Ambrose Federal Detention Center had to be handled differently since 27 prisoners were housed in three groups of nine each. The AFDC had been chosen as the detention site primarily because it was already rigged for such a situation. Each of the cell blocks had been constructed with a delivery system that could flood the area with an oneirogenic general anesthetic in the event of riot or disturbance.

Oneirogenic general anesthetic is the formal name for sleeping gas, an incapacitating agent used to place a subject in a state of unconsciousness so that they are not aware of what is happening around them. Often it is used to keep a person from harming themselves or others. Most sleeping gases have undesirable side effects and are only effective at doses that approach toxicity. The gas used in this situation was odorless, colorless, and tasteless so as not to alert its victims.

When the atmosphere was purged, medical teams entered and checked the unconscious men. Portable oxygen was administered to each flushing their lungs. IVs were attached to the right arm and right femoral artery of each prisoner. The 27 patients were transferred to the main gymnasium area where four "operating tents" stood; within each was a surgery team. Two anesthesiologists rotated among the patients, checking on their individual statuses.

Alone in solitary confinement, Captain Dodd stood suddenly and looked widely around the room. His observers noted the time. His apparent agitation continued to increase periodically; his observers continue to make notes and keep track of the exact times each increase occurred. This had been anticipated.

Exactly two hours and twenty-three minutes later, Captain Dodd stopped pacing and stood stock still. The only movement was the periodic shift of his head from side to side, like a dog trying to determine what a particular sound was or where it was coming from. Fifteen minutes after it had started, the behavior ceased and Captain Dodd sat back down.

*****

John Thomas and Paul were seated on Rourke's patio. The events of recent days were troubling. "Excuse me Paul," Rourke said. "I need a bit of a distraction." He returned a few minutes later with a box of knife sharpening tools and two knives.

Before the Night of the War started, Rourke was traveling between assignments and passed through a Texas border town. His friend, Hank Frost, had told him about two fledgling knife makers, Ed Martin and his son Newton, Newt for short. Rourke was working on two knife designs, and if there was anything the one-eyed mercenary knew about, it was knives. Frost told him to "Check these boys out; they can make them. I guarantee it. Here's the address. Why don't you stop and see them on your way out?"

Rourke pulled his black Ford pickup into the parking spot outside the shop and walked inside. Over a cup of scalding coffee, he learned that Newt was a submariner home on leave from the Navy; his father Ed and his uncle Hank had been "playing" at knife making for years. Playing meant they made good quality using knives, but were still "playing with our own designs" as Newt told him.

"I have a couple of ideas I'd like you to look at," Rourke said as he pulled two sheets of paper from his bomber jacket pocket and laid out two rough designs, "I'm not locked into very many specifics. I want to see what you come up with. To quote Jim Bowie from the Iron Mistress, 'I've seen guns fail. I've seen swords fail. I want something that won't fail,' and I want two of them. One needs to be a Bowie fighter and the other a spear point dive knife, small enough to carry concealed if necessary but big enough and strong enough to hang my life on if need be."

"What do you have in mind?" Newt asked.

"Roughly this," Rourke said. "The Bowie fighter first, I want it out of high carbon steel. I haven't found a stainless blade that sharpens or holds an edge like high carbon. I want it out of quarter-inch stock with integral guards top and bottom. It will need to have some 'very aggressive' serrations and a skull crusher at the end of the handle with a thong hole. Lastly, the handle needs to be of the type you can fight with the blade upright or a reverse grip."

"You must live an interesting life, Mr. Rourke," Ed said from the work table.

"You could say that Mr. Martin," Rourke agreed with a wry smile. "I seem to keep running into people who don't like me. I was referred to you by Hank Frost; we're sort of in the same business, just different bosses."

Ed rolled his eyes, "That explains a lot; give my best to Hank. Did he ever tell you the true story about how he lost that eye?"

Rourke smiled, "He's told me about 15 different stories, and I didn't believe a one of them."

Newt said, "The dive knife should be stainless for corrosion resistance. It definitely needs serrations and a wire break. We can make it with a reversible friendly grip, with a thong and crusher also. I like the spear point idea; I don't care for the pry bar types with what looks like a big screwdriver for a point."

"Me either," Rourke agreed.

"What about sheaths?" Newt asked.

"Leather for the Bowie and not chrome tanned. That will rust the blade, maybe eight or nine ounces," said Rourke. "Do you guys have any experience with the new plastic sheathes that recently came out?"

"I know what you're talking about, but it is referred to as Kydex, not plastic," Newt said.

"I'll need one of those for the dive knife, and I'd like one out of leather for when I'm not underwater."

"What about blade length?" Newt asked, while he was taking notes.

Rourke thought before answering, "Like I said, I may need to conceal them, so... What are your thoughts, five to six inches long? I want to be able to carry it conventionally on my belt or mounted horizontally in the back."

"I want to work on the blade geometry," Newt said. "But, I think that is doable."

"Whatever you come up with will be fine, but I want them as visually similar as possible. The two knives will make a set. And, I'd like this mark on both knives." Rourke took Newt's pencil, sketched out a design, and slid it across the work table.

Newt stood up and went to a cabinet, "Let me show you one dive knife I've been working on for a friend who is a commercial diver." Opening a drawer, he pulled out a T-shirt wrapped bundle and opened it. Rourke took a look, handling the knife; he liked the balance and heft of it. "Newt," he said. "This is close; this is very close."

Ed slid his chair back and stood up, "Mr. Rourke, how long are you going to be in town?"

Rourke glanced at his watch and said, "It will be about another hour if you guys will let me buy you lunch. Then, I'm headed out to the Panhandle to meet with Hank; he has a little 'project' he needs some help on. If you think it's enough time, I can pick them up on my way back through in about two weeks; just tell me the price."

Newt and Ed looked at the drawings and spoke for a moment before deciding, "Two weeks will be pushing it for both knives and the sheaths; a month would be better."

Rourke shook his head, "Can't do a month fellas, I might be able to give you a couple of extra days, but as soon as I'm finished with Hank's project, I leave for at least two months overseas. I understand if you don't want the project."

Ed sized Rourke up before asking, "What are you thinking for lunch?"

Rourke saw this as an opening, "If you boys can do it, I'm buying steaks."

Ed looked at Newt, "Whatcha think, Son?"

"It will be tight, but I think we can do it," Newt said rubbing his face.

"Alright," Ed said, if you don't mind us putting our mark on the backside of the blade. Heck, who knows, this knife might be famous one day. Get out your checkbook Mr. Rourke; we're walking about two blocks to Mother's Cafe, finest Texas chicken fried steak in town." With a handshake, the deal was sealed.

Two weeks and three days later, Rourke had taken possession of the knives. The father and son team had exceeded his expectations. He had only used the knives once before placing them in his retreat in Georgia. He never saw the Martins again. Three months later, the end of his world began. Rourke was returning home from Canada; his airliner was diverted and forced to make a controlled crashed-landing in New Mexico, with Rourke at the controls. The day of the crash was when he first met Paul Rubenstein, a bespectacled nerd and a book worm. A geek with no training or abilities except one, he was willing to learn, and he wanted to survive. He had done both!

Rourke had recently found the knives again, while he was going through boxes salvaged from the retreat. "I don't know why I haven't carried these more," he said to Paul. "These would be great replacements for situations in which the Crain LSX is simply too big." He laid the two Martin blades on the table along with the A.G. Russell Crock Stick and a half dozen other knives. The Crock Stick unit held two nine-inch long "alumina ceramic" sticks that attached to an oak wood base, ten inches long and two inches wide, at the correct angle to sharpen almost any type of blade. Rourke liked to use it to finish a sharpening.

The angles involved in blade sharpening were well known; edges with less than 10 degrees were reserved for edges that are typically cutting softer materials. In this case, the edges are not subject to abuse, so the lower angle can be maintained without damage or edge failure. The lowest angles are typically on straight edge razors; those have a very delicate edge that is very easy to damage. In proper usage, a straight razor would never see the type of use that would damage the edge.

Angles of 10 to 17 degrees are still quite low for most knives, making the edge typically too weak for any knife that might be used in any type of chopping motion. Also, consider that harder steels are also more susceptible to impact damage because they are more brittle.

Most kitchen knives have a 17 to 20 degree angle. Some knives (typically Japanese manufacturers) will sharpen their knives to roughly 17 degrees, while most western knives favor roughly 20 degrees. Most pocket or hunting knives will fall into the 22 to 30 degree angle range. The knife edges are considerably more durable, and while they inevitably see abuse not seen by knives meant primarily for slicing or chopping softer materials, they are considerably more durable. A machete, cleaver, or axe must be durable as the typical cutting action of these tools would damage other edges; these usually carry about a 30 degree edge.

Rourke also favored Norton India Combination Oil Stone with two grits, fine and coarse. One side is used to restore slightly dulled cutting edges. He used the coarse side to sharpen dull edges quickly. Paul had picked a small Arkansas Hard Rock out of the box. He was touching up the edge of his pocket knife, letting Rourke's mind and the conversation run free.

"Paul," Rourke said, "when I was giving my lectures on survival, I tried to get over to people the necessity of planning ahead, which included going armed on a road trip. There are a thousand situations and locations where you could run into trouble on the road, one of the big ones being rest areas, especially after dark. I'm a firm believer that avoiding trouble in the first place is a lot better than shooting your way out of trouble."

"I know what you mean," said Paul. "Long drives can be boring; it's easy to tune out for a while. You can lose your situational awareness."

Rourke nodded, "Reminds me of an old friend of mine, Hank Frost, you would have liked him, Paul. Old one-eyed former Green Beret drummed out after he lost his eye. He did a lot of mercenary work back in the days before the Night of the War. He always said, 'When you pull into a rest area, scan the area, particularly at night, and park in lighted areas away from other vehicles. Scan the area where you will be headed before you ever get out of your car. If you are going to get a snack out of the vending machines, have just a few bucks out of your wallet beforehand and leave the wallet in your pocket while you buy your snacks.' Of course, that was when we still had rest areas along the inter-state highways, but you get the idea."

"Yes, all of that makes sense," Rubenstein agreed and smiled. "Here's an-other tip; I'm right-handed. I keep my right hand free AND above the urinal on the wall; I pull my zipper down with my left hand. That way, should someone come up behind me and shove me forward at a urinal, both hands won't be locked against the porcelain or the wall. I keep my strong hand up, so I can strike or grab my weapon instead of just holding my privates."

Chapter Forty-Three

The flight back to the KI had taken only a few moments. The shuttle pilot had not spoken, and The Keeper had no idea what to say and no inclination for conversation. Once the shuttle had docked, The Keeper stood to disembark. The pilot turned and said, "Your presence has been requested by our Captain. He's asked that you come directly to him."

The Keeper nodded and proceeding down the stairs where he saw an escort waiting for him. *This is most unusual*, he thought. He was taken to the Captain's personal quarters. "I am glad you have returned Keeper; you have been away for too long. Much has happened in your absence."

"Thank you, to what do you refer?"

"Sit, we must talk," The Captain indicated a chair. "May I have refreshments brought for you?"

"Thank you, no."

The Captain nodded and began, "There are issues and circumstance you are not aware of. There are changes that have occurred while you were gone. Some of them you may be troubled by until I explain them."

"Proceed," The Keeper looked at the Captain with a great respect.

The Captain cleared his throat nervously before saying, "As I said, there have been changes... many changes."

The Keeper interrupted, "Captain, you are repeating yourself. What has happened? What has changed?"

The Captain was not an individual at all familiar, or comfortable, with the level of intimidation he felt being in his old teacher's presence. "Yes, you are correct. I am repeating myself. First of all, our leader's health has suffered while you were absent. His physicians are not hopeful; they fear his passing could come at any time."

"I am sorry to hear about my old friend; when you are finished with me, I shall go see him," The Keeper said with genuine concern etched on his face.

"Yes, do that," the Captain said. "Now, let me get to the rest of the reasons I wanted to speak with you. As you know, our leader is the last of his lineage;

the Council has decided it is time for changes in our form and style of government."

"That is not unexpected," The Keeper said.

The Captain nodded his agreement, "It is not. I fear that it is, however, coming at a most difficult time. I would like your opinion on something."

"Certainly," The Keeper said. "How may I be of assistance?"

"I am concerned that our return to Earth is going to meet with... unnecessary resistance."

"Really, I am not sensing that in my conversations with Earth's leaders. In fact, I believe that they are actively seeking our support; and frankly, their response to me has been welcoming, generous, and open."

"Yes," said the Captain. "And, I would like for you to continue in your efforts. However, for the good of our own people and in an effort to reestablish our position in the order of things... I believe we should be making preparations should their attitudes change. I don't believe we should ignore the potential for problems to develop, with governments we have no direct influence with. In that vein, while you were gone, I have reached out myself through our emissaries, and I am pleased to report we are making strides to a different alliance."

"Is that why my shuttle pilot was armed?" The Keeper asked. "Is that why I've seen some of your people on board armed?"

"Yes," the Captain smiled. "I have found a people who share our views and are willing to provide resources to help in the attainment of our goals."

The Keeper frowned, "Captain, is it not possible that you have been processing all you saw and heard against your internal dialogue and comparing and judging everything. Let's take a look at that. Now, I am certain that you believe you were listening, but in fact, it may also be that you were simply just running the sounds of the day against your own inner dialogue, the beliefs and preconceived notions that you hold."

The Captain could feel himself growing somewhat defensive and replied, "Well, isn't that how we and these humans process our experiences? We look at what we think about things, what our own experiences have taught us, and evaluate what the other person is saying?"

The Keeper responded, "Well, that is one way to process experiences. You spend a large amount of your mental energy evaluating what they have said and deciding if it is 'right' or 'wrong.' That leaves you actually listening with only a portion of your mental capability. The human ego is so busy doing its thing; we miss much of what is actually happening. What did you see on my face when you looked at me for my reaction to the other speakers?"

"You seemed to be just listening. There didn't seem to be any reaction," the Captain replied.

"That's right. I was just listening. I had shut off all of the internal noise, so I could be present in the discussions." The Keeper went on, "Who was doing the listening in your head?"

The Captain said, "Well, I was. Who else could be?"

The Keeper smiled, "And, who was watching you analyzing all that was occurring?"

The Captain looked puzzled and asked, "What do you mean?"

The Keeper replied, "While you were running all of your ego oriented judgments, was there not a part of you watching all of your mental programs and listening to your inner noise?" The Keeper went on, "So, where or who is the real you? Is it the part of you that maintains the mental noise, or is it the watcher who simply sees all the noise and doesn't place any positive or negative value to the thoughts?"

"You are not your thoughts. You are not your judgments. In many ways, you are not even your beliefs, although they can determine the direction of your day-to-day reality." At this, The Keeper paused for a moment.

"I will assure you of this; it will take constant awareness on your part to start to realize this new way of experiencing physical reality. The apparent 'separateness' or 'us and them' is a strong underpinning of physical reality itself. Very few humans have any memory of when they may not have been physically incarnate, and their greater instinct is to continue to experience life as they always have. It is a habit, perhaps one that we could stand to lose or change." Once again, The Keeper paused, as if to let the Captain digest what he had been sharing.

"Your conscious mind was developed to help you make decisions that would maintain the integrity of the physical body while in physical reality. The body needed a portion of the mind that could focus intently on what was in the immediate experience of the person. It would keep us from danger and learn from previous experiences. Such as, I noticed that the lion ate Uncle Henry. I probably should avoid being around lions in an unprotected way in the future."

"Unfortunately, the conscious mind, many times referred to as the Ego, took on the responsibility of not only protecting the body's integrity and longevity but also its own. It was developed to assist us with the apparent separation that comes with being physically manifest; but, it started comparing itself to others and forming judgments and polarities. It started developing levels of separateness in our perception so that now we have an incessant, uncontrollable chatter continually going on in our mind."

"It has progressed to the point that very few humans are actually present in their day-to-day lives. They are simply continually running the inner dialogue in their mind and actually miss the majority of what life is offering in the moment." At this, The Keeper stopped talking.

The Captain sat down with his head bowed, attempting to follow The Keeper's words. Inside, they felt right to him, but how does a person live that? What happens if we stop judging some as right and others as wrong? Surely, the Alien Greys were wrong, and the Humans were right!"

The Keeper thought to himself, *You have found people who share your views, and they are saying they will help in the attainment of your goals. I fear, my Captain, you are already making a deal with the Devil.*

The Keeper kept these thoughts to himself and said instead, "Captain, I fear I am somewhat light-headed after my journey. With your permission, may we continue this talk after I have rested?

"Certainly, are you alright?"

The Keeper nodded and made a point of rising from the chair with a bit of a wobble, "I suspect it is the differences between the gravity on Earth and what we are used to here. I'm sure I will be fine after a short rest. May I return to my quarters, and may we speak tomorrow?"

"Certainly," the Captain said. When the door to his quarters slid open, The Keeper noticed his escorts outside. He turned and said, "My dear Captain, I assure you I know the way to my quarters, but thank you for the escort. They will not be necessary however."

The Captain nodded and dismissed them, "Be well my old friend. Be well."

"And you," The Keeper said stopping just outside the door and turning back. "One thing Captain; in my time on Earth with these people, I have learned theirs is a history filled with violence, intrigue, and death. It is also a history filled with great beauty, accomplishments, and knowledge. Their cultures are definitely different from ours, and those differences are somewhat oblique and difficult to define, as is their language. Be careful, my friend; alliances with them should be based on knowledge, performance, and ethics and not simply on statements of well-being and agreement."

The Keeper turned and walked slowly to his quarters, alone and fearful of what tomorrow and all of his tomorrows might now bring.

Chapter Forty-Four

Rourke remembered dreaming many dreams that night but could not pull any of them up into his conscious mind the next morning. They swirled in and out of his consciousness, never actually manifesting; the only constant seemed to be they all involved The Keeper. He lay in bed and knew he needed to gather his thoughts; it was then he felt a "gentle probe" in his mind. He shook his head to clear it, but the probe again tickled his awareness.

Barely a whisper at first, less than an impression and more like a mental breeze—a thought began to form in John's mind, *Yes John, it is me; lie back down and close your eyes.* Rourke shook his head again, *Trust me John; please lie back down and close your eyes. The first contact is always the most difficult.* Rourke did not understand what was happening to him; was he finally losing his mind? The answer came unbidden to him, *No John, you are fine. Relax, so I can reach you.*

"Keeper," Rourke said aloud and laid back down closing his eyes. "Is that you?"

Yes John, I am sorry I did not discuss this possibility with you before contact became necessary.

"How?" Rourke asked. "What is happening?"

It is a gift some of my people have; seldom is it practiced anymore. It became unnecessary due to our close quarters during our journey. It is only practiced today by certain few of my people. I look forward to more discussions with you in the future; I hope you will allow it. As you have said, the connection between you and I has always been strong, and I had thought to discuss it with you at another time later; now, it is imperative that I make contact with you.

"Imperative," Rourke said aloud. "What has happened?"

It is better John if you do not speak aloud. Simply think what you want to say; speaking aloud makes our connection difficult. It is like you are shouting at me.

Rourke thought, *I'm sorry; is this better?*

Yes, John, see how simple it is?

Rourke smiled, *Yes, I have heard about telepathy before but never experienced it. Can you read my mind also?*

No John, that would be invasive and unethical. Once I have established the link, we just talk to each other. I promise your thoughts are your own. It is only possible for me to attempt contact with another's mind. That person must be willing to accept the contact for us to communicate. It is not possible for either of us to pry into the others' thoughts. It is only possible to visit as we are doing.

Rourke frowned, *What has happened? Why have you made contact with me like this, and why now? Are you alright?*

Yes, my friend, currently I am alright. But, I fear circumstances within my people have changed.

Rourke pulled a tablet and pen from the night stand; *Go ahead; I'm going to take notes if that is acceptable with you?*

Yes, I have much to convey to you, and I do not know how long I will have.

Rourke had always believed that, because of all his medical and CIA operative training, he would have developed a calmer more "still" mind; but, he had never contemplated something like this. The Keeper spoke again in his head. Rourke did what The Keeper had suggested and pulled himself back from the thoughts and just let them flow by like clouds instead of trying to identify, justify, or disprove them.

He began to see that he was as infected with a running mental commentary as any others. He had judged his abilities as being more "correct" or more "evolved" than others, but he began to see he did the very same thing. He began the process of identifying his internal mental dialogue and attempted to stop feeling that the dialogue was in some way him. They were just random thoughts, nothing more, nothing less.

Rourke wrote furiously, while The Keeper spoke to his mind. Finally, The Keeper said, *Excellent, I am happy for your learnings. You may find that the desire to once again immerse yourself in the mental chatter will arise. It is a long developed habit, and it gives the Ego great peace to know it is in charge and contributing so much good will to your life. It can be a long and tedious path to step back out of the mental chatter and to just let it pass by and not*

identify with it. For most of your life, it has been one of your closest compan-
ions, and as the saying goes, 'Old habits die hard.'

With this, The Keeper said, *I will leave you now, but I must warn you this*
first contact will probably have some physical impact on you. We have seen
that before. Relax, it will pass shortly. We will talk again, I fear sooner than
later. Until next we meet again my friend, provided we do meet again. Then, he
was gone. Rourke sat up in the bed and placed the tablet and pen aside. He
found he was shaking and covered in sweat. He called out to Emma; she came
running.

"John, what's the matter with you?" Emma cried out when she stepped into
the room.

"Emma," Rourke said wiping sweat from his face. "Sit down; I have had
the most incredible experience." As he told the story, Emma's hand flew to his
lips.

"Honey, do you hear what you are saying?"

"Yes," he said with a nod, "I know what it sounds like, but what I'm telling
you is true. I need you to call Michael and Paul; I need to speak with the whole
family right now. I'm going to take a shower to wash this sweat off. Tell them
to arrange for the kiddos and get here as soon as they can."

*****

Michael and Natalia were the first to arrive with Paul and Annie, pulling into the
drive before they had exited their vehicle. Two carloads of Secret Service
agents parked along the curb. Rourke, in a heavy bath robe and slippers, was
still towel drying his hair. Emma had poured him a stiff drink, and he already
had half of it downed.

"Come on in guys," Rourke waved them into the living room. Michael, the
first to speak asked, "Dad, are you okay? Your color isn't normal."

"Son, that's because I have just had a most unusual experience," Rourke
said. "But yes, I'm okay; I'm just a little weak and shaky."

"What happened, John?" Paul asked steadying Rourke as he walked him to
the easy chair. Rourke smiled, took another slug of the whiskey, and said,

"There was a time when I held out great hope for mankind. While I'm still optimistic in some areas, I've had to make adjustments in others. Our great age of philosophy is considered to have been during the time of the ancient Greeks. Our great industrial age moved civilization forward more rapidly in 100 years than it had in 100 centuries. Our great technological age pushed scientific advancements to incredible heights. Then, mankind almost destroyed everything."

"While our spirits can soar to great heights and our minds conceive great things and we have the capacity for great good and beauty, it is the flaws of our basic nature that makes us capable of our own destruction. I saw it in my own time before the Night of the War. I saw it when we awoke 500 years later that, whereas we had been strong enough and smart enough to pull civilization out of the cesspool my time created, little had changed. Even after our second sleep, when I awoke, little had changed."

"Now, we stand poised on the brink of a gambit that mankind might not survive this time. The old evils are still common in our species. Greed, the hunger for power, the need to control, and the wish to dominate must be hardwired into our DNA the way our skin color is. The more that we learned humans were equal to each other, the more some people tried to destroy or subjugate the rest of mankind."

"Countries against countries I can understand. Threats must be dealt with for your own survival, but we seem hell-bent to move from crisis to crisis without pause. Each brings us closer and closer to destruction, and one day, we will be successful and destroy ourselves. There has never been a weapon created that was not used, not once. And each time, it was hoped the creation of that weapon would make war so terrible that we would stop fighting; we never have. I don't believe we ever will."

"I saw that people are pretty much the same, no matter what country I was in. The average person just wants to raise their kids and live in peace. People are people are people. It is when ideologies, passions, religions, and governments get involved that it all turns to crap; and people, sometimes entire civilizations, are wiped out."

"There is a psychopathic strain in us that allows many to justify, and even sanctify, their evil ambitions and desires. An evil person with charisma and evil intentions will always find weaker folks to follow them, and it always ends up ugly. I have often thought my life had progressed like I was dancing a two-step. Two steps forward and one step back, and my dance partner is stepping back two steps and coming forward one. Neither of us are able really to gain a lasting advantage; maybe, in reality, that's all there ever really is. Life, I guess, is just that: a dance; the trick is to try and be graceful during it."

"Dad," Annie said, "I think we have all felt like that from time to time. I know I certainly have, but what is this all about?"

"Annie," Rourke said, "I think we have just reached a singularity, an event so stunning, so unexpected, so out of the ordinary... And, I have been told something that could alter everything we think we are doing."

"What was the 'singularity' you're talking about? What happened?" Paul asked.

"Guys," Rourke said hesitantly, "you're not going to understand this or believe it. Hell, it happened to me, and I don't understand it; but, I do know it really happened." For the next 45 minutes, Rourke spoke without interruptions, often referring to the notes he had taken. At the end, he asked simply, "Well, do you believe me or not?"

Paul was the first to speak, "John, this is incredible. However, ever since you and I first met, the incredible has been a part of our lives; I believe you."

"Thanks, Paul," Rourke said. "How about the rest of you?" They all nodded.

"Okay, Dad," Michael said, "you described this experience as 'a singularity,' an event so stunning, so unexpected, and so out of the ordinary that it could alter everything we think we are doing. What does that mean to you?"

"Michael," Rourke said shaking his head, "to be honest, I'm not sure at the moment. The Keeper did not explain everything to me, and there is a lot I don't understand yet. I do know this; there are things happening in the KI community that The Keeper is extremely uncomfortable with. He is sharing that discomfort in the hopes that a great tragedy can somehow be averted. He believes it is possible but will require great effort on both parts. He is also concerned there will be forces actively involved in assuring our efforts will be unsuccessful."

"I know this," Rourke continued. "When he was picked up by his shuttle craft, the pilot was carrying a side arm. Seeing that weapon had a visceral impact on him because his people do not have that kind of weaponry. It had a visceral impact on me because I've seen that type of weapon before and so have each of you." Rourke paused for effect, "It was a Russian energy pistol."

Michael lowered his head, "Oh crap, not those guys again."

Natalia put one arm over her husband's shoulder, "That ties to what we learned about the Russians who took Paul hostage. We knew there was some reason for them appearing again, but I never saw this coming."

John Rourke finally stood, still a little shaky but definitely stronger now. "First rule; this conversation, and this information does not leave this house. Right now, we might have a little edge, a very small edge, but that edge could be extremely important in the days to come."

Chapter Forty-Five

The next afternoon Rourke was returning from the store when he felt the probing again. Recognizing the feeling, he pulled into the parking lot of a shopping mall, drove to the far end, and parked. *Hello, John; is this a good time?* The Keeper spoke to his mind.

Shutting off the vehicle, Rourke answered, *Yes, it is.*

Good, how are you feeling? The Keeper asked.

The effects only lasted about an hour, John answered.

Good, The Keeper said. *You should find this conversation much easier with less discomfort.*

Rourke pulled his note pad out, *That is good,* he thought. *Yesterday was pretty tasking.*

As I told you, each subsequent connection is less... traumatic, I believe is the correct word.

What is going on? Rourke asked.

Changes, The Keeper said. *Massive changes in the fabric of the KI society. As I told you yesterday, the ability to make this type of contact is something that all KI had at one time. The discipline, however, has fallen into disuse and is only practiced by those in what we refer to as the Seneia; you would call it a Senate of Scholars and Philosophers.* The Keeper continued, *Things have changed up here just during the period I was contacting the Wild Tribes. There is now a militaristic slant that is being imposed by the Captain on our activities.*

Rourke thought for a moment before framing a response, *What kind of slant?*

We now have weapons being worn in plain sight; there are escorts for members of the Seneia wherever we go. Excursions to your world can now only be authorized by the Captain. Our leader is in very poor health, John. My estimates are he is within the last days of his life. If I am accurate, the Captain has positioned himself and his force to render massive changes in our culture. The Keeper was silent for what John thought was a long time.

Are you still there? Rourke asked.

Yes John, I'm still here.

Rourke thought The Keeper was searching for his next words. Rourke finally said, *The weapon your shuttle pilot was carrying I recognized; I've seen similar ones carried by Russian forces we call Spetsnaz. They are elite Russian assault forces. Apparently, that confirms our suspicions about KI involvement at the village massacre.*

The Keeper finally spoke, *Yes, I have no longer any doubt about that. The questions I have are what does this all mean, and do we have the ability to intervene in what I believe are nefarious ambitions on the part of the Captain? Unfortunately, John, I have little experience in the ways of scoundrels and intrigue. What should I do?*

First of all, Rourke thought, *It is absolutely essential that we maintain our communications and the secrecy of those communications. As yet, we have suspicions from our side of the equations, but you may very well be the only hope we have to prove those suspicions. You are probably our only hope to get advanced information that can prevent a cataclysm for your people and mine.*

You realize, John, The Keeper said after another long pause, a*cting against my people in deference to the survival of yours is not something I would be capable of doing. Traitorous acts are not within my makeup.*

Rourke took a deep breath, *You do not have experience by your own admission in 'the ways of scoundrels and intrigue'; I do. It was the aggression of the Russians that destroyed my world over 650 years ago. Their thirst for power is unquenchable; their penchant for deceit is unimaginable and their ability to be trusted does not exist. Whatever agreements the Captain has made, I promise you will not be honored. Whatever game he believes he is playing, he is wrong Keeper. Trust me; he is being played by an opponent who has had centuries of experience in the art of lies and manipulations. Their goals have not changed since the end of our own Second World War; their defeats from time to time have only served to enslave new peoples who heard what they wanted to hear and made the mistake of believing the Russians were capable of honor and the truth.*

Rourke took another deep breath. He could not push too fast or too far with The Keeper without driving him away, something neither society could afford to have happen. *Is it possible for you to return to Earth?* Rourke finally asked.

It may be; I have already laid the groundwork to return and finish my studies with your people.

Is the Seneia a body that you can trust? Rourke asked.

No, I cannot trust the Seneia, as a body, but there are those within the Seneia I do trust.

Rourke thought for a moment before asking, *Will you have the ability to mentally contact those you have trust in the way you have contacted me?*

Yes. The Keeper answered.

Good, very good, Rourke thought. *Then, do whatever you have to do to get back down here but be able to have contact with your own people. It is imperative that I have the opportunity to show you some things, but it is equally imperative we have the ability to communicate with people you trust up there. Do you have any feel for how long it will take for you to get back down here?*

If, and that is a big question, if I can get back, it will take me two days to prepare.

Good, that will give me time to gather what I'll have to show you. You are certain that this form of communication is protected from prying eyes or I should say minds?

Yes, John, right now that is about all I am sure of.

Rourke nodded to himself and thought, *Then, begin the process and keep me posted.*

Be well my friend; we'll talk soon. With that, The Keeper broke the connection.

Rourke noticed that he was barely sweating and was not shaking at all. He felt clearheaded and even slightly rested. He called Paul, "Are you available for a short conversation?"

"Did your friend call again?" Paul asked.

Rourke smiled, "Yes, he did; we just got 'off the phone.'"

"All is well?" Paul asked.

"No, not well, but it is not a crisis yet. I'm going to need your help; how's the research on the book coming?"

Paul hesitated, "The book?" he finally asked. "Do you mean our diary?"

"Yes," Rourke said. "Swing by the house this evening; I have an idea."

"Will do."

*****

Paul arrived a little after 6:00 p.m. "What have you got, John?"

"I don't have solid proof yet, but it appears that the KI being known as The Captain has established contact with the Russians and has entered into some type of pact with them. The Keeper is not sure what agreements, or for that matter that any agreements, have been made, but it appears so."

"That is definitely not a good thing," Paul said.

"No, it is not," Rourke agreed. "However, in addition to that little tidbit, it appears the KI are about to change leaders. The current one is in poor health, and The Keeper does not think he will survive very much longer. The Captain is positioning himself for what The Keeper believes will be a takeover of power. Now, the next question is, with that gain of power and with the consolidation of activities with our Russian friends, what does that mean for our own people?"

"Well, we know what that has meant in the past, don't we?"

"Yes," Rourke said. "And, the best predictor of future behavior is past behavior. I see no reason to suspect, or even entertain, the possibility that the Russians have turned over a new leaf."

Chapter Forty-Six

The armored sedan carrying Acting President Jason Darkwater pulled quiet-ly into the circular drive of the White House. Darkwater exited and walked directly to the door that led to the Presidential Library, knocked once, and entered. Inside were the President and the leaders of the Lockout Teams. "Mr. President, gentlemen," Darkwater said and took his seat at the conference table.

"Thank you Jason," Michael Rourke said. "I appreciate you coming."

"Not a problem, Mr. President. Honestly, I was not expecting action yet."

"Okay, gentlemen," Rourke said with a sigh, "the imperative for Lockout has changed. While the original concern about a traitor conspiracy remains of the upmost importance, here's the situation; I have come into some information. At the present, I'm not at liberty to divulge how I came into this information, but I assure you the source is impeccable."

Daniel Hasher spoke, "Gentlemen, when the President briefed me on this information, I activated certain 'technical' assets' of our electronic and systems surveillance; you know them as the 'hacker squad.' That team has been able to penetrate communications in the Extremely Low Frequency bands. As you all know, ELF or sub-radio frequencies have a variety of uses, not the least of which is to communicate with submarines and other submerged targets."

"Due to its electrical conductivity, seawater shields submerged targets from higher frequency radio waves, making radio communication with those sub-merged targets impossible. Signals in the ELF frequency range, however, can penetrate much deeper. There are two factors which limit the usefulness of ELF communications channels: the low data transmission rate of a few characters per minute and, to a lesser extent, the one-way nature due to the impracticality of installing an antenna of the required size on a submarine. The antennas need to be of exceptional size for the users to achieve successful communication. Generally, ELF signals were used to order a submarine to rise to a shallow depth where it could receive some other form of communication."

"In other words, effective ELF communications are extremely limited and the transmissions difficult to capture, unless you are monitoring that exact frequency at the exact time of the transmission. However, our satellites are capable of monitoring and recording all radio transmissions at whatever frequency. Review of those recordings, now that we know what we were looking for, have detected radio transmissions from a here-to-for unknown source off the coast of the Kamchatka Peninsula that were directed toward the KI fleet in geo-orbit above the continent of Antarctica."

Darkwater frowned, "How is it possible from an ELF transmission in the northern hemisphere to contact the KI fleet on the underside of the planet?"

"The message was actually bounced using our own satellite system," Hasher said. "It was ricocheted around the world. The messages were in the frequency range of 0 to 300 Hz; these wavelengths in air are very long, 6000 km at 50 Hz and 5000 km at 60 Hz; and, in practical situations, the electric and magnetic fields act independently of one another and are measured separately."

"Why are we just now finding out about this?" Darkwater said.

Rourke spoke, "Before I came into this information, we did not know we were looking for anything. The messages were invisible because we weren't looking for them."

Hasher continued, "This type of communication is not only what we use to communicate with our submersed ships, but it is the exact system that was used by the old Soviet/Russian Navy using SIASs or Submarine Integrated Antenna Systems. In any event, once I knew to look for something, we found it and the location from where the communications originated. This enabled us to confirm and validate the information the President is talking about."

Darkwater nodded, "And, I assume we have now identified linkage with the KI?"

Rourke nodded, "Affirmative, we have tracked shuttle activity between the KI and the Kamchatka Peninsula. We also have been able to locate communications between a submerged vessel that left that area and appeared for a short time off our coast, then departed. The timelines indicate they probably disembarked the suicide team that took Paul Rubenstein hostage."

Retired Rear Admiral Hank Sanders, past Director for the Farragut Technical Analysis Center, said, "As Captain Hasher said, this is old technology we are familiar with, but we have never seen it used in this manner. But now that we are aware, we're on top of it."

"So, what's the next step, Mr. President?" Darkwater asked.

"It is apparent there has been some sort of Russian outpost we did not know about before. It is apparent there has been contact between the KI and that outpost. It is apparent some type of alliance is being forged between that outpost and a faction of the KI that is directed at us."

"'Us' being the United States?" Darkwater asked.

"No, Jason," Rourke said. "'Us' being the human race."

Darkwater stood, "What now Mr. President?"

Derek Billings spoke for the first time, "We are putting together a joint operation of both land and undersea forces. The undersea branch will be disguised as normal naval operations that just happen to be in the area. We had training exercises already scheduled and simply moved the area we'll conduct them in. The land operation will be a penetration and insertion onto the Kamchatka Peninsula. If all of the members of the Lockout agree, we will identify, contact, and hopefully eliminate that Russian threat once and for all."

Rourke spoke again, "We suspect there is an element of the Russian Spetsnaz and Navy that we did not know about, possibly in a facility similar to Mid-Wake that has operated invisibly since the last defeat of the known Russian army almost 20 years ago."

"When do we move?" Darkwater asked. "Gentlemen, I believe it is time for us to vote and make our recommendations to the President. All in favor of initiating this plan..."

All raised their hands. Darkwater turned to Michael Rourke, "Mr. President, do I have your permission to initiate?"

Rourke looked at each person in turn, lowered his head, and spoke a silent prayer before speaking, "Yes, Jason. Initiate."

Darkwater walked to the President's desk, picked up his phone, dialed a number, and said simply, "Initiate." Turning back to the group, he asked, "When do we go?"

Billings checked his watch before answering, "My team leader and his team are currently on standby awaiting our instruction. Their briefing will begin in 15 minutes."

Darkwater nodded, "Alright then, now where are we standing on the conspiracy?"

Chapter Forty-Seven

The Military Weather Intel Specialist from the Office of Naval Intelligence began her briefing, "Maritime influences are most pronounced with annual precipitation which can reach as high as 98 inches, while the southeast coast south of Petropavlovsk-Kamchatsky generally receives around 53 inches of rainfall equivalent per year. Considerable local variations exist; southern parts of the Petropavlovsk-Kamchatsky metropolitan area can receive as much as 17 inches more than the northern part of the city. Temperatures here are very mild, with summer highs no more than 59°F and winter lows around 18°F, whilst diurnal temperature ranges are seldom more than 9°F due to persistent fog on exposed parts of the coast. South of 57°N, there is no permafrost due to the relatively mild winters and heavy snow cover, whilst northward discontinuous permafrost prevails. Be glad the operation is occurring now."

"The west coastal plain has a similar climate, though rather drier with precipitation ranging from 35 inches in the south to as little as 17 inches in the north, where winter temperatures become considerably colder at around −4 °F. Immediately offshore along the Pacific coast of the peninsula runs the Kuril-Kamchatka Trench which is 34,400 feet deep. The Kuril-Kamchatka Trench or Kuril Trench is an oceanic trench in the northwest Pacific Ocean. It lies off the southeast coast of Kamchatka and parallels the Kuril Island chain to meet the Japan Trench east of Hokkaido. It extends from a triple junction with the Ulakhan Fault and the Aleutian Trench near the Commander Islands, Russia, to the intersection with the Japan Trench."

"The trench formed as a result of the subduction zone that formed in the late Cretaceous, which created the Kuril Island as well as the Kamchatka volcanic arc. The Pacific Plate is being subducted beneath the Okhotsk Plate along the trench, resulting in intense volcanism. Now, for your specific purposes, be advised there is a road from Bolsheretsk to Petropavlovsk and another from this road up the central valley with a bus service to Ust-Kamchatsk. The northern end of the road is of poorer quality. Apart from the two roads, transport is by small plane, helicopter, four-wheel drive truck, and army truck."

Pointing at a place on the graphic, "This obvious circular area in the central valley is the Klyuchevskaya Sopka, an isolated volcanic group southeast of the curve of the Kamchatka River. West of Kronotsky Point is the Kronotsky Biosphere Reserve with the Valley of Geysers. At the southern tip is the Southern Kamchatka Wildlife Refuge with Kurile Lake. There are several other protected areas: Palana is located in the Koryak area on the northwest coast and Opala volcano in the southern part of Kamchatka. There is considerable variation, however, between the rain-drenched and heavily glaciated east coast and the drier and more continental interior valley."

"In the interior valley of the Kamchatka River, represented by Klyuchi, precipitation is much lower at around 18 to 26 inches, and temperatures are significantly more continental, reaching 66 °F on a typical summer day and during extreme cold winter spells falling as low as −42 °F. Sporadic permafrost prevails over the lower part of this valley, but it becomes more widespread at higher altitudes; glaciers or continuous permafrost prevails north of 55°N. The summer months are popular with tourists when maximum temperatures range from 59 to 68 °F, but a growing trend in winter sports keeps tourism pulsing year-round. The volcanoes and glaciers play a role in forming of Kamchatka's climate, and hot springs have kept alive dozens of species decimated during the last ice age."

*****

Sanderson's men had been taking copious notes; on his signal, they moved to a terrain mockup of the area they would be landing on. Planning was everything in an operation like this; almost anything could go wrong, and according to Murphy's Law, "If something can go wrong, it will go wrong and always at the worst possible time."

Epilogue

The penetration team led by Marine Chief Warrant Officer 2nd Class Wes Sanderson consisted of 22 Special Warfare Operators plus John Thomas Rourke and Paul Rubenstein, both part of a very small group that had fought both old Soviet Union forces and remaining Russian forces after the Night of the War. They had been inserted three nights before by a High Altitude Low Opening parachute drop, known as a HALO.

By the third night, there had still been no contact with the enemy. Rourke walked over to the campfire and sat down next to Sanderson, "Mr. Sanderson, I have been studying you. You're what I would call a 'little different,' aren't you?"

Sanderson said, "I suppose I am; is there anything wrong with that?"

"No," Rourke said. "I don't mean anything negative by that comment. I'm a little different also. Actually, I embrace that difference. There are very few people I would want to be like. I was just wondering what your story is."

"My story," Sanderson said. "What do you want to know?"

"Well for one thing," Rourke said, "your speech patterns are not familiar to me. Where are you from? I don't believe you are from the States, are you?"

"No, not originally," Sanderson said. "I am a naturalized American citizen; I'm adopted. My birth parents came from what your people call the Gallia. I was born to one of the Wild Tribes of Gallia. After the Night of the War, our people were reduced to a few scattered family units trying to survive, and our civilization returned to the savagery of the ancients. My father was the leader of our clan, and we led a hard and brutal life."

"When I was 13, a group of strangers came to our land; they were archaeologists led by a gentleman, Dr. Wesley Sanderson. They stayed with our clan for almost six months and studied our people, and Dr. Sanderson told us stories of what he thought our history might have been. I particularly liked his stories about the Sarmatians, an ancient people that flourished from about the fifth century BC to the fourth century AD. They spoke Scythian and Indo-European languages of the Eastern Iranian family."

"Their territory, which was known as Sarmatia, corresponded to the western part of greater Scythia, later known as the modern Ukraine and Southern Russia all the way to a smaller extent of the northern eastern Balkans around Moldova. At their greatest period of expansion, around 100 BC, these tribes ranged from the Vistula River to the mouth of the Danube and eastward to the Volga. They bordered the shores of the Black and Caspian seas as well as the Caucasus to the south."

"They were nomadic Steppe land fighters; skilled with bow and spear from horseback. Supposedly, they were descended from the Scythians and the Amazons. That Amazon legend was widely accepted among Greeks and later, Romans and Sarmatian women had a much higher social standing than their Mediterranean counterparts."

"The Sarmatians also had a near religious fondness for their swords; one worship process involved a sword sticking up from the ground. This could have been the foundation for the 'sword in the stone' story tied to King Arthur. The bravest of their people took the title 'Narts' which some historians suggest may have evolved into the English word 'Knights.' There is even a story about a magical woman dressed in white, and somehow associated with water, who helps the hero acquire his sword, similar to the Arthurian Lady of the Lake."

"Three days after he and his party left, our clan was attacked by a neighboring clan. I was on a hunting trip and returned too late. My village was destroyed, the smoke still rising from the fires that only a few days before had been our homes. I found my father dead and my mother dying. She told me to leave and find Dr. Sanderson, and then, she died."

"After burying my family, I set out on horseback to find his team. Four days later, I came across his camp and told him what had happened. Sanderson opened not only his heart but his home to me. Upon his return, Dr. Sanderson formally adopted me, hence my name. My birth name is almost unpronounceable in English, so he gave me his. He always called me Adam. My adopted father and mother never had children of their own. They gave me the middle name of Adam; that's what they always called me. They taught me your language and made sure I was educated with a classical orientation. Their graciousness gave me a new name, a new family, and a new life. He enrolled me in school and 'civilized' me. Years later, I had just turned 18 and was away at college when my adopted father and mother were on another archaeological encampment with the wild tribes, and he was killed by a marauding band of butchers."

"I dropped out of college and joined the Marines. I guess, somehow, I wanted to avenge his death, but by that time, I had already decided that his world of academia was not for me. I needed more action; the Marines gave me that and more, more direction and more challenge. You could say I had rein-vented myself once again. That was when I stopped using my middle name and went to Wesley."

"This is all I have left from that old life," Sanderson said as he removed an amulet from around his neck and handed it to Rourke. It was a piece of carved antler about two inches long and an inch wide. One side had been flattened, and on the flat, someone had carved the head of a horse; its mane stood out behind the head, flowing as if it were racing.

"This is beautiful," Rourke said. "How did you come by it?"

"My birth father carved it for me when I was about 10," Sanderson said re-claiming the treasure and placing it around his neck again. "I have no idea who my people really were; my adopted father's stories about the Sarmatians were upon my favorites, so I adopted their legends as my own. I've always had an ear for languages, and that has helped me in my new career. Anyway," Sander-son said, "that's my story, not much of one. I am the last of my clan; I have no more history, no more foundation for my life except what I remember from my childhood and what I assimilated from stories."

Rourke smiled, "I think you've done pretty well, Mr. Sanderson."

In that instant, the night exploded around them with impact detonations and energy blasts ripping the fabric of the night. Sanderson hollered, "Sparks, get on the radio!"

Sparks, the radioman, was already broadcasting on the special frequency they had been assigned, "We are taking fire. I repeat, we are taking fire."

Rourke's last sardonic thought was *The Russians are coming. The Russians are coming.*

*****

Over 5,000 miles away in Göbekli Tepe Turkey, Natalia Tiemerovna-Rourke, former Major in the Russian KGB and current First Lady of the United States, was in the fight of her life, and she knew she wasn't winning. What had started out as a peaceful archeological dig looking for evidence of a prehistory contact with an alien race exploded into a full-blown attack by unseen forces. Six of her security protective detail and four of the archeologists were down already; half of them appeared dead.

The radio used to maintain contact with the outside world had taken a direct hit in the first moments of the attack; it sat at her feet smoking, a useless jumble of components. At first, she had feared the attack was from the alien race. Next, she feared it was a Russian force, either of which would probably have been an improvement over the reality. They were under attack by a marauding band from one of the Wild Tribes of Gallia. These guys were armed with semi and full automatic weapons; but as advanced as that appeared to make them, they still ate the captives. Their lucky victims were dead before the process took place; the unlucky, Natalia did not want to think about that...

Author's Note: Bob Anderson

When my friend Jerry Ahern called and asked me what I thought about resurrecting John Thomas Rourke and THE SURVIVALIST series, I was excited. THE SURVIVALIST was my favorite series long before I met and got to know Jerry and his wife Sharon. I told Jerry I would help in any way I could. We brainstormed and I started doing some research for him. We discussed several story lines, little realizing how important that research would be to me in just a few months.

After Jerry's untimely death July 24th, 2012, his wife, Sharon, asked me to join her in bringing the series back—an honor I never imagined. The task of bringing John Thomas Rourke back to life was daunting. Jerry's story lines, several going on simultaneously in each book, his attention to detail, his knowledge of tactics and weapons, all combined to form the most demanding and challenging writing assignment I ever received.

As the project developed, a decision was made to form a new company. Rourke readers should recognize the name **LANCER** from the original series. It is the firearms company that the Rourke family had "loaned" their 20th Century weapons to so that "faithful" reproductions could be made. The name **LANCER** is just another "wink" at the genius of Jerry Ahern.

Sharon Ahern, a driving force throughout the process, sits on the Board of Directors. For the first time ever, John Thomas Rourke items, knives, and memorabilia will be offered to the loyal readers of the original series and to new fans. These items are currently under development and each will be reviewed and approved by the authors.

Jerry and I had done some concept work on a new set of knives for John Rourke, specifically a BOWIE FIGHTER and a SPEAR POINT that could double as a dive knife. Both had to be small enough to carry concealed if necessary; but, in Jerry's words, "Big enough and strong enough to hang my life on if need be". I reminded him of Jim Bowie's quote from the movie, *The Iron Mistress*—"I've seen guns fail. I've seen swords fail. I want something that won't fail." Jerry's responded, "Exactly, and I want two of them."

We decided the BOWIE FIGHTER should be made out of high carbon steel, with a five to six-inch blade. It needed to be made out of quarter-inch stock with integral guards top and bottom. It would need "very aggressive" serrations, as well as a skull crusher at the end of the handle as well as a thong hole. Lastly, the handle needed to be of the type you can fight with, the blade upright or a reverse grip.

The SPEAR POINT DIVE KNIFE was to be made of stainless for corrosion resistance. Like the BOWIE FIGHTER, it had to have a reverse friendly grip, also with a thong and crusher. The leather sheath for the BOWIE was to be leather and designed to be hung down from a belt or mounted horizontally in the small of the back or set up for cross draw.

Jerry's last stipulation was, "Whatever you come up with will be fine but I want them to be as alike as possible. Yes, they will be two different types of knives, but I want them to be a set." I worked up the JTR (John Thomas Rourke) brand below to be placed on both blades.

13168072R00119

Printed in Great Britain
by Amazon.co.uk, Ltd.,
Marston Gate.